dish

friends, cooking, eating, talking, life.

Deep Freeze

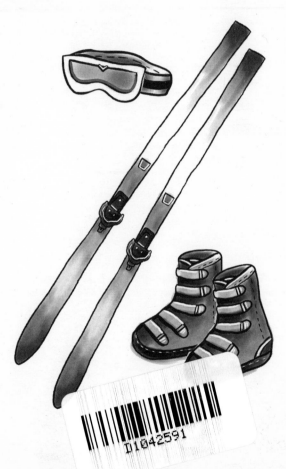

...ser & Dunlap

GROSSET & DUNLAP
Published by the Penguin Group
Penguin Group (USA) Inc., 375 Hudson Street, New York, New York 10014, U.S.A.
Penguin Group (Canada), 90 Eglinton Avenue East, Suite 700, Toronto, Ontario,
Canada M4P 2Y3(a division of Pearson Penguin Canada Inc.)
Penguin Books Ltd, 80 Strand, London WC2R 0RL, England
Penguin Ireland, 25 St Stephen's Green, Dublin 2, Ireland
(a division of Penguin Books Ltd)
Penguin Group (Australia), 250 Camberwell Road, Camberwell, Victoria 3124,
Australia(a division of Pearson Australia Group Pty Ltd)
Penguin Books India Pvt Ltd, 11 Community Centre, Panchsheel Park,
New Delhi - 110 017, India
Penguin Group (NZ), 67 Apollo Drive, Mairangi Bay, Auckland 1311, New Zealand
(a division of Pearson New Zealand Ltd)
Penguin Books (South Africa) (Pty) Ltd, 24 Sturdee Avenue, Rosebank,
Johannesburg 2196, South Africa

Penguin Books Ltd, Registered Offices:
80 Strand, London WC2R 0RL, England

Cover photo © Veer

Library of Congress Cataloging-in-Publication Data

Muldrow, Diane.
 Deep freeze / by Diane Muldrow ; illustrated by Barbara Pollak.
  p. cm. -- (Dish ; #12)
 Summary: The Chef Girls are excited about the seventh-grade ski trip, which is filled with snow
sports and practical jokes, but when Shawn's nemesis Angie plays a prank that goes too far, things
take a dangerous turn.
 ISBN 978-0-448-44693-6 (pbk.)
 [1. Skis and skiing--Fiction. 2. Bullying--Fiction. 3. Middle schools--Fiction. 4. Schools--Fiction. 5.
Friendship--Fiction.] I. Pollak, Barbara, ill. II. Title.
 PZ7.M8894De 2007
 [Fic]--dc22
                    2007004942

10 9 8 7 6 5 4 3 2 1

dish
#12

Deep Freeze

...ends, cooking, eating, talking, life.

By Diane Muldrow
Illustrated by Barbara Pollak

Grosset & Dunlap
New York

For little Mason, and her mom, Kerri—D.M.

chapter 1

"Amanda! Amanda! Over here!"

Amanda Moore glanced around Windsor Middle School's large auditorium, trying to see who was calling her name. Suddenly, she spotted her friends Peichi Cheng, Shawn Jordan, and Natasha Ross down in the front row. Peichi was standing on her toes, waving wildly, trying to attract Amanda's attention.

Amanda grinned and waved back, then tried to make her way toward them. The entire seventh-grade class had been herded into the auditorium for a special assembly, and the narrow aisles were packed with kids laughing, shouting, and shoving one another as they tried to sit with their pals. From the back of the auditorium, Amanda finally shrugged helplessly at Peichi, as if to say, "I can't get down there!" Peichi made a small pouting face, and Natasha nodded understandingly.

"Manda!"

Amanda knew exactly who was calling her now—her twin sister, Molly, who was sitting at the opposite end of the row to Amanda's left. Amanda saw that the row had already filled up except for a single seat next to Molly, which her twin had protectively blocked off with her heavy backpack.

"Sorry, sorry, oops, excuse me, sorry," Amanda mumbled as she squeezed down the aisle. *"Phew!"* she exclaimed as she flopped into the seat next to Molly. "Thanks for saving me a seat."

"No prob," replied Molly. "I tried to get down to the front, too, but there was no way. It's packed!" Suddenly, Molly burst out laughing. "Did you see that? Someone just threw a paper airplane and it hit Natasha in the head!"

"Ohmigosh!" giggled Amanda as she watched Natasha turn around to find the culprit. "Did you see who did it?"

"Nope. I would have figured it was Omar, but he's onstage," Molly said. "Oh, wait—it had to be Connor! He's been almost as big a pain as Omar ever since Omar was elected class president."

Amanda could tell that Peichi, Shawn, and Natasha had figured the same as Molly. They were whispering together as Peichi crumpled up the paper and got ready to throw it at Connor Kelly, who was sitting a few rows directly behind them. But before Peichi could toss it, Mr. Degregorio walked onstage and stood in front of the girls. Natasha grabbed Peichi's arm to stop her just in time!

"Nice save!" cried the twins. They exchanged a glance and started laughing. They were doing the "twin thing" again—saying the same thing at the same time—which happened a lot!

Teachers patrolled the aisles, trying to quiet the rowdy students. A big assembly and a Friday afternoon were a bad combination for getting anyone to sit quietly. But when Principal Wagner walked to a podium onstage and tapped the microphone, a hush quickly fell over the students.

"Welcome, seventh-graders!" Principal Wagner said in her loud, upbeat voice. She was a short, stocky woman in her mid-fifties whose elegant business suits made her stand out among the teachers. "I'm sure you're all wondering why we're here today..."

"I know why," Amanda whispered in Molly's ear. "Evan told me on the phone last night. It's the..."

"I know," Molly whispered back, interrupting Amanda before she could continue. "You already told me." Ever since Amanda had gone on a date with the cute eighth-grader Evan Anderson, she acted like she knew everything about what was supposed to happen in seventh grade.

"We're here to talk about..." Principal Wagner paused for effect. "The seventh-grade ski trip!"

The auditorium erupted into cheers and applause. Principal Wagner grinned at the students, then raised her hands for quiet.

"Each year, after completing the unit on colonial life, the seventh-grade class spends Presidents' Day weekend at

Chestnut Hill Farm in Vermont, an actual farm from the eighteenth century that is still run largely like it was over two hundred years ago! Besides having an opportunity to ski, sled, and snowboard—" Principal Wagner paused as the students started screaming again, "—you'll get to work on a real farm, the way colonial settlers did!" She paused again, smiling brightly, waiting for the students to cheer. The twins exchanged a glance. Something about working on a farm just wasn't as exciting as going skiing!

Principal Wagner cleared her throat. "Yes. Well, I'd like to ask the seventh-grade class officers Omar, Iris, Tessa, and Mark to pass out the informational packets now. Please read them with your parents over the weekend. We'll be having a meeting for your parents next week to answer any questions they might have. But before school lets out for the weekend—" Principal Wagner was interrupted by more cheers. "—do any of you have questions? No? Okay, then please stay seated until the bell rings. You may talk quietly with your neighbor."

As soon as Principal Wagner stepped away from the podium, everyone in the auditorium started talking and laughing excitedly. Molly and Amanda grinned at each other. "This is going to be so awesome!" exclaimed Molly. "I love skiing!"

"And we've never been to Vermont!" agreed Amanda.

The bell rang then, and the twins—like everyone else

in the auditorium—jumped out of their seats, ready to start the weekend.

"Shawn! Let's meet at the trophy case," Molly hollered over the noise in the auditorium. Down in the front row, Shawn nodded and gave Molly and Amanda the thumbs-up sign.

It took about five minutes for the twins to get out of the auditorium as the crush of students slowly made its way through the double doors. A few minutes later, the girls met up in the front hall.

"Everybody ready to brave the cold?" asked Natasha, wrapping her fuzzy scarf around the lower part of her face. The girls nodded, bracing themselves for the blast of icy air when they opened the doors.

Normally, when the five friends walked through their Brooklyn, New York neighborhood of Park Terrace, they chatted and laughed the whole way. But today they walked quickly and quietly through the icy wind. This January had been the coldest one on record.

Park Terrace seemed to have everything, with its dozens of delicious restaurants that served food from all over the world, its unique stores and cool boutiques, and its beautiful botanic garden. Plus, there were movie theaters, an ice-skating rink, and enormous Prospect Park, which had thick woods, a nature center, and rolling meadows that were perfect for summer picnics. Best of all, Park Terrace was only a short subway ride away from Manhattan, the heart of New York City! But during the coldest weeks of winter, most residents tried to stay indoors, going outside only for school, work, or trips to the grocery store.

The girls soon arrived at the Moores' spacious brick townhouse on Taft Street. Molly was fumbling in her backpack, searching for her keys, when suddenly the front door swung open. Mom was home early!

"Come in, come in," she exclaimed, holding the door open wide. "I've got a pot of cocoa on the stove. Let's get you girls inside and warm you up!"

"Thanks, Mrs. Moore," Shawn, Natasha, and Peichi chorused as they pulled off their hats, gloves, scarves, and coats in the front hall.

"What are you doing home already, Mom?" asked Amanda as she hung up her cranberry-colored parka. "Don't you teach a four o'clock class on Fridays?"

Mrs. Moore smiled. "I do—but it was cancelled today! Brooklyn College closed at three o'clock because of the winter storm warning," she explained. "Did you see that sky? We'll be having a snowstorm, for sure."

"Ugh!" groaned Peichi. "This is the third weekend in a row where it snowed on Friday. Why can't the storms just wait until Monday? Then *we'd* get a snow day, too!"

The girls laughed as they followed Mrs. Moore down the hall. The sweet aroma of hot cocoa filled the cheery kitchen, the twins' favorite room of the house. The warm yellow walls were complemented by beautiful blue and green tiles Mom had bought in Spain, and scrolled iron hooks from the ceiling held gleaming copper pots and pans. Cupboards with glass doors displayed Mom's collection of colorful dishes, and a large baker's rack against the wall held everything from cookbooks and potted herbs to a large mixer and a funny pitcher shaped like a cow. The twins couldn't think of a better place to hang out with their friends and family.

"Matthew, stay away from the stove," Mom said in her "warning" voice to the twins' eight-year-old brother, who was leaning over the pot of simmering cocoa.

"Sorry," Matthew mumbled. "It smells so *good*!"

"It sure does!" Mom said with her loud laugh, reaching over to rumple Matthew's brown hair before he could duck out of her reach. "Buddy, I think there's a bag of marshmallows in the pantry. Would you check for me?"

In a flash, Matthew darted out of the room to look for the marshmallows, startling the family's fat tiger cat, Kitty. Mom started ladling the creamy cocoa into seven large mugs. "So, what is Dish cooking tonight?" Mom asked.

"It's an easy job," Peichi spoke up. "Just two breakfasts and two dinners for Mr. Peterson, who lives on my block. We're gonna make blueberry muffins, a big pot of porridge, lasagna, and chicken potpie."

Dish was a cooking business that the five friends had started during the summer before sixth grade. It all started one boring day when Molly and Amanda were stuck at home, sick of eating the take-out food their busy parents kept bringing home for dinner. Molly had the great idea that the twins should surprise their family by cooking dinner for them. Even though Amanda had been hesitant to cook an entire meal from scratch, it had been a huge success—and it tasted great! Soon, the twins were taking cooking classes at Park Terrace Cookware with Shawn, where they ran into Peichi and Natasha.

When the class ended, the girls started a cooking club, which quickly turned into a cooking business they called Dish. Many families in Park Terrace were just as busy as the Moores, and loved having the option of calling Dish for some delicious, fresh meals, instead of the same old takeout or frozen food. The Chef Girls, as they called themselves, were surprised by how quickly their business had taken off. Suddenly, they were catering fancy parties, appearing on TV, and helping others by fund-raising and donating food.

"I was planning to make tacos for dinner tonight. Would you girls like to stay?" Mom asked.

"Sure!" chorused Shawn, Peichi, and Natasha.

"Let me just call my mom to see if it's okay," Natasha added, tucking her chin-length blonde hair behind her ear. She ducked into the den to use the phone.

"Hi, Mom?...School was good. Um, Mrs. Moore invited everyone to stay for dinner. Can I?" *Please, Mom,* she thought. *Say yes!*

"Well..." Mrs. Ross paused. Natasha could almost see her mother's expression—she was surely biting her bottom lip as she thought. Mrs. Ross could be pretty strict, and she usually liked to have more notice about Natasha's plans.

"The rest of the girls are staying. I'll come right home afterwards, I promise," Natasha added, crossing her fingers.

"Well, sweetie, it's just that I wanted you to practice for your bat mitzvah tonight," said Mrs. Ross.

"Oh, right. Well, I should be home by seven. Is it okay if I practice then?"

"All right," Mrs. Ross finally agreed.

Natasha breathed a sigh of relief. "Thanks, Mom! I'll see you in a couple hours. Love you!"

"I love you, too," Mrs. Ross replied before hanging up the phone.

Natasha returned to the kitchen, where her friends were drinking their hot cocoa. "I can stay!" she announced.

"Yay!" cried Peichi.

"Oh, Mom! Guess what!" exclaimed Molly, slapping her forehead. "We had an assembly today about the seventh-grade class ski trip!"

"How exciting! Tell me about it!" Mrs. Moore replied.

"It's over Presidents' Day weekend," Molly began.

"We're going to a farm in Vermont to see how colonial settlers lived," Amanda broke in. "There's a meeting next week for parents to get more information."

Mrs. Moore walked over to the large calendar on the wall where she and Dad kept track of the family's busy schedules. "Great. When is the meeting?"

"Tuesday night," Amanda replied, pulling the neatly folded flyer out of her pocket. "Seven o'clock."

"I've never been skiing before," Natasha said.

"Oh, my dad and I love skiing," Shawn said. "We haven't been in a while, though."

"Remember that ski trip we went on?" Molly asked Shawn. "That was great. What was that—four years ago?"

"Five," Amanda corrected her sister. "We were in second grade, remember?"

"Right. Oh, hang on, I'll be right back!" Molly raced to the living room where Mom kept all of the family photo albums. She flipped through a few until she found the one she was looking for, then returned to the kitchen. "Check out these pictures!" she said with a laugh. "We were so little!"

Everyone gathered around Molly as she opened the album, which was full of pictures from the vacation the Moores and the Jordans had taken to Mount Snow, New Hampshire.

"*Awww!* You guys are so cute!" Peichi cooed. "Shawn, you're adorable with your glasses!"

"I had just started wearing glasses," Shawn remembered with a smile. "I hated them!"

"Look at the twins in their snowsuits!" giggled Natasha as she glanced at a photo of Amanda in a pink-and-silver snowsuit with her arm around Molly, who was wearing a plain red one. "Even then they had their own styles."

"That's for sure," said Molly, rolling her eyes. "I remember Amanda wanted us to have matching snowsuits that year, but I *refused* to wear that pink thing!"

As everyone laughed, Amanda shook her head and poked her sister playfully. "I should have known then that Molly was a lost cause!"

Though Molly and Amanda were identical twins, it had always been easy to tell them apart. The twins had the same pale skin and freckles, bright green eyes, and long brown hair, but their styles were completely opposite. Amanda was the fashion-conscious twin. She kept up with all the latest styles and loved anything girly and glittery. Molly was more into casual, comfortable clothes. She preferred high-top sneakers to high-heeled boots, and jeans to jewelry.

Everyone paused at a family photo of the Jordans.

"Shawn, is that your mom?" Natasha asked hesitantly. "She's so beautiful."

"You look just like her," Peichi said softly.

Shawn stared at the picture of herself as a child, standing between her parents. In the picture, Shawn was smiling at the camera. Mrs. Jordan was laughing, and Mr. Jordan was smiling affectionately at her.

After a moment, Shawn cleared her throat. "Yeah. This trip was...was right before my mom found out she was sick," she said, trying to sound normal. "We didn't know..." Her voice trailed off as she thought, *We didn't know so much—that she was already sick, that she was going to die...*

Uh-oh, Molly thought, embarrassed. *Why did I bring out that album? I should have remembered it had pictures of Mrs. Jordan!*

Across the table, Amanda was sending Molly a worried glance. Then her voice cut through Shawn's thoughts. "You okay?" she asked lightly, putting her hand on Shawn's arm.

Shawn tried to smile at her friends. "Yeah. Sorry, guys. I was just...I was surprised to see that picture."

"Would you like to keep it, sweetheart?" Mrs. Moore asked gently. "It's a beautiful picture of your family."

Shawn thought for a moment, then nodded. "Thanks. I would like it—if you don't mind."

"Not at all," Mom replied as she slipped the photo out of its plastic sleeve.

Just then, Matthew came barreling into the kitchen, carrying a thick album over his head. "I want to look at these pictures!" he announced. "These are my favorite ones." He dropped the heavy album on the table with a loud *thud* and opened it. On the first page was a picture of Mrs. Moore, hugely pregnant, taking the twins to school on the first day of kindergarten.

"I still can't believe I was so huge!" Mom exclaimed. "You were a big baby, Matthew!"

"Wow. Is that what *my* mom is gonna look like?" Peichi asked. Peichi had been an only child for twelve years, but in a few months, that was going to change—her mother was expecting a baby!

"I was so jealous when Matthew was born!" Shawn admitted with a smile. "I wanted a baby brother or sister so badly. I thought it would be like having a really cool doll to play with. But the very first time I held Matthew, he spit up in my hair!"

As everyone laughed, Matthew protested, "No I didn't! I would never do that!"

"Oh, yes, you did," teased Amanda. "You threw up on *everyone*—Mom, Dad, Molls, me, Aunt Livia, Poppy. We used to call you Splat-hew!"

Matthew's face turned red as everyone laughed again.

"Don't get upset, Matthew," Mom said nicely. "The twins were barfy babies, too—and there were *two* of them!"

"Yuck!" cried Peichi. "I hope our new baby isn't a barfy baby! That's gross!"

"Better a barfy baby than a fussy baby," Mrs. Moore said wisely. "Some babies just cry and cry and cry—no matter what you do, you can't quiet them down."

"Oh, no," Peichi moaned. "What have my parents gotten us into?"

"Don't worry, Peichi," Amanda said. "You can just move in here if you get stuck with a fussy, barfy baby!"

As everyone laughed again, Molly cleared her throat. "Well, let's get to work," she said. "This job will be so easy that maybe some of us should help Mom make dinner."

"Yeah, no problem! Especially since I might be moving in soon!" joked Peichi.

Molly, Shawn, and Natasha split up the Peterson job—Natasha took over breakfast, making a pot of hearty, filling porridge and a tray of scrumptious blueberry muffins; Shawn made the lasagna; and Molly put together the chicken potpie. Mom directed Amanda and Peichi on the tacos. Mom fried some tortillas in hot oil until they were golden and crispy, and Peichi browned the ground beef with minced onions and chili powder. Amanda washed and chopped tomatoes, lettuce, olives, and made guacamole with some ripe avocados. Matthew helped, too, by grating some cheddar cheese. When he thought no one was looking, he snuck a bite.

"Something smells delicious!"

Mr. Moore stood in the doorway, still wearing his heavy parka. The creases of his jacket were covered with fine, powdery snow, and his graying hair was wet and matted with melting snowflakes.

"Mike! Look at you! You're covered in snow!" Mom exclaimed.

"It's not so bad," Dad replied. "The snow's sticking out there, but the flakes are very small."

Mom brushed the snow off Dad's coat and fluffed up his wet hair. "This is perfect ski snow," she said over her shoulder to the Chef Girls.

"Skiing? Who's going skiing?" Dad asked as he wiped off his glasses.

"We all are!" exclaimed the twins. "The seventh-grade class is going on a ski trip over Presidents' Day weekend," Amanda added.

"That's fantastic!" Dad said. "Now, if you'll excuse me, I think I'll go warm up—and dry off—before we eat. Right now, I feel like the abominable snowman!"

"Hurry up," Mom called after him. "These tacos will be
 ready to eat in about five minutes—and they smell so good that I don't know how many we'll be able to save you if you're not down here!"

After dinner, Peichi called her father to pick her up. Since she lived right down the street from the Petersons, it would be easiest for Peichi to deliver the food and pay everyone on Monday. "Natasha and Shawn, do you guys want a ride?" she asked. "My dad says it doesn't make sense for your parents to come out in the snow, too."

"Sure," Shawn and Natasha said. "Thanks!"

Twenty minutes later, Mr. Cheng arrived. "Sorry it took so long," he said. "I had to drive very slowly—the visibility is terrible out there!"

"Thanks for taking everyone home, Andrew," Dad said.

"Drive carefully!" added Mom.

After their friends left, Molly and Amanda started talking about the ski trip. "I cannot *wait* for this trip!" Amanda exclaimed. "It's gonna be totally amazing!"

"Me, too!" Molly said.

"Hang on a minute, girls," Dad replied. "We need to talk about this trip a little more. It's going to be expensive—especially to send two of you."

"You're right, Dad," Amanda said. "I didn't think of that."

"Of course, we want you to go and have a great time!" Mom said quickly. "But we need to talk about this."

"Hey, how about we chip in some of our own Dish money?" Molly suggested.

"That's a great idea," Dad said. "Mom and I can cover the rest."

"But—I mean—Christmas just ended!" Amanda wailed. "I spent all my money on presents. I don't have *any* saved up."

"That's because you always blow it on CDs and makeup and stuff," scolded Molly. She turned to Mom and Dad. "Would you loan Amanda some money for the trip? She could pay you back out of future Dish jobs."

"I don't see why not," Mom agreed. "Does that sound okay to you, sweetie?"

"Absolutely! As long as I get to go on the trip!" Amanda exclaimed.

On the drive home, Peichi, Shawn, and Natasha chatted excitedly about the ski trip. Peichi couldn't wait to get home to tell her mother about it.

"Mom, Mom!" she yelled.

"I'm upstairs, Peichi!" Mrs. Cheng called from her bedroom.

Peichi found her mother reading in bed. "Mom! Guess what! The entire seventh-grade class is going on a ski trip! Isn't that amazing? It's over Presidents' Day weekend and it's in Vermont and we'll be doing all kinds of cool things that colonial settlers used to do like farming and cooking and stuff and I really want to bunk with the Chef Girls—" Peichi paused to take a deep breath.

"How exciting! You're going to have a great time!"

"Yeah! I can't wait! We haven't been skiing in a couple years. I hope I remember how! Do you think I will? Is it like riding a bike?"

Mrs. Cheng laughed gently. "I'm sure it will come right back to you, Peichi. But we'll need to buy you some new ski clothes. I can't imagine that your old parka and snow pants from fourth grade still fit!"

Peichi laughed with her mom. "Plus, that parka has a dumb-looking bunny on it! It's seriously babyish."

"If the storm clears up by morning and it's not too cold, perhaps we can go shopping tomorrow. Dad and I need to start buying things for the baby's room, too."

Peichi clapped her hands together. "Yay! Thanks, Mom! I'm so excited! Do you think your old skis will fit me?"

"Let's go check!" replied Mrs. Cheng. "All of that stuff is in the attic. And some of your old baby clothes, too!"

Peichi grinned at her mom, then bounded up the stairs. "Come on! Let's go!"

"Hey, no fair!" called Mrs. Cheng, laughing. "Slow down!"

"Oops, sorry, Mom!" Peichi said. "I forgot..."

"Don't worry," Mrs. Cheng said. "In a few more

months, I'll be able to keep up with you—and your new baby brother or sister!"

When Natasha got home, she found her parents sitting quietly in their elegant living room.

"Goodness, Natasha," exclaimed Mrs. Ross. "Your cheeks are bright red! It must be *freezing* out there!" Mrs. Ross hurried over to Natasha and pressed her smooth, perfectly-manicured hands against her face.

"It's *really* cold," Natasha said. "Oh, you lit a fire! Oh, that's perfect!" She wriggled out of her winter clothes and hurried over to sit by the hearth.

"Let me get you something warm to drink, sweetheart," Mr. Ross said. "Would you like some hot apple cider? Or cinnamon milk?"

"Cinnamon milk would be great," Natasha said, smiling at her father. She loved the lightly-sweetened warm milk he'd made for her at bedtime since she was a little girl, with its comforting blend of cinnamon and vanilla.

Mrs. Ross joined Natasha in front of the fire with a thick, leather-bound notebook in which she'd been keeping all the information about Natasha's bat mitzvah and the huge party that would take place afterwards. In a little over a month, Natasha, who had just turned thirteen, was going to be bat mitzvahed at her temple. She was very excited about the ceremony that would mark her transition to womanhood in the Jewish religion—but also a little nervous. The thought of reading from the Torah, the first five books of the Bible in Hebrew, in front of an entire room full of people, made her anxious.

The guest list was sticking out of Mrs. Ross's binder. *I wish Mom and Dad hadn't invited, like, the entire world. What if I mess up when I have to read from the Torah? I hate the thought of all those people watching me!* Natasha stifled a sigh. *Having all their friends at my bat mitzvah is really important to Mom and Dad,* she reminded herself. *And it's really nice for them to throw this huge party for me. Anyway, the invitations went out weeks ago. It's too late to worry about it now.*

Mrs. Ross seemed completely unaware of how nervous Natasha felt. "Oh, Natasha, this is so exciting!" she exclaimed. "I can't believe you're going to be bat mitzvahed! It seems like just the other day that Daddy and I picked you up at the agency and I held you in my arms for the first time!"

Natasha's heart started beating faster. Just a few years ago, she'd been shocked to learn that she had been adopted as an infant—and even more shocked that her parents had kept it a secret for over ten years. Even after the truth had come out, her parents had still been reluctant to talk about the adoption.

Just then, Mr. Ross returned to the living room, carrying a tray with three blue porcelain teacups of steaming cinnamon milk and a plate of gingersnaps.

"Thank you, David," Mrs. Ross said, reaching for a cup. "Now, Natasha, let's go over your portion of the Torah."

"Oh, wow!" Natasha suddenly exclaimed. "I can't believe I almost forgot to tell you! Guess what!"

"What?" asked Mr. Ross.

"The seventh-grade class is going on a ski trip to Chestnut Hill Farm in Vermont over Presidents' Day weekend!" exclaimed Natasha. "It's going to be fantastic!"

Mr. and Mrs. Ross exchanged a worried glance.

"It's, um, it's an educational field trip," Natasha continued. "We've been studying colonial life, and now we'll get to see firsthand how the settlers lived."

Still, her parents said nothing. Finally, Mrs. Ross spoke. "I don't think so, sweetheart," she said, shaking her head. "Skiing is *very* dangerous. You don't tolerate the cold well. And that's just a week before your bat mitzvah. What if you catch a cold? Or break your leg? To be honest, Daddy and I aren't comfortable with you going away without us for such a long time."

Natasha's mouth dropped open. "Are you *serious?*" she gasped. "It's only four days! And everybody else is going!" She looked at her father for support, but he glanced away.

21

"Yes, I'm serious," Mrs. Ross replied, her lips set in a thin line. "Besides, you don't *know* that everyone else is going. I'm sure many parents will feel as Daddy and I do."

"No, they won't!" Natasha exploded. "Why are you doing this? You didn't even hear what I had to say about the trip! It's an *educational* trip!"

"Let's—" Mr. Ross began, but Mrs. Ross cut him off.

"Natasha, I'm sure you can learn lots about colonial life without going on a ski trip. Now, I've given you perfectly good reasons why I don't want you to go on this trip. Daddy and I said *no*. End of discussion."

"No!" Natasha yelled. "This is something I really want to do. All of my friends are going. Practically the whole *school* is going! You don't have a single good reason for saying no, Mom! I'm not a baby anymore—stop treating me like one!"

"Don't take that tone with me, young lady!" Mrs. Ross raised her voice. "Your behavior shows us that you aren't mature enough for a trip like this."

Tears pricked at Natasha's eyes. "I'm *sick* of you always getting in the way and ruining my life!" she cried, jumping up. As she turned to run upstairs, Natasha caught a glimpse of her parents' upset faces. She tried to ignore the guilty feeling in the pit of her stomach. *But everything I said was true!* Natasha thought angrily. *She is always getting in the way!*

Once she got to her bedroom, Natasha slammed the door behind her and pulled her journal out from under her mattress. Writing down her thoughts and feelings almost always made her feel better—but tonight, Natasha didn't think she'd quickly forget the hurt look on her mother's face.

When Natasha awoke the next morning, her face was puffy and red from crying. *That was the worst night of sleep ever*, she thought. Every time Natasha remembered what she'd said to her mom, her face flushed in embarrassment. *I wish I hadn't been so mean. But why does Mom always have to be so strict? It'll be so embarrassing if I'm the only kid in seventh grade who can't go...but yelling at Mom won't help anything.*

With a sigh, Natasha made the decision to apologize. Natasha slowly walked downstairs, where she found her parents talking quietly in the kitchen over their coffee. They both fell silent when Natasha entered the room.

Natasha took a deep breath. "Um, listen," she began. "I'm sorry about last night—the yelling and the things I said. I didn't mean it. I felt really bad all night." She looked down for a moment, and when she looked back up, her parents were smiling warmly at her.

"Thank you, Natasha," Mrs. Ross said, rising from her

chair. Her voice sounded a little stiff, as if she was still upset, but she gave Natasha a kiss on the cheek. "I'm sorry, too."

"I still want to go on the trip," Natasha said quietly. "But I know you guys have to do what you think is best."

"Thanks for apologizing, sweetheart," Mr. Ross said warmly. "That's very mature. We'll try to work something out so that everyone is happy."

"Thanks, Dad," Natasha replied. She started to fix herself a bowl of cereal. *I wish they knew how much I want to go on the trip,* Natasha thought. *I wish they weren't always so overprotective.*

At the Jordans' house, Shawn and her dad were just finishing breakfast. "That was some delicious French

toast, baby," Mr. Jordan said as he started clearing plates from the table. "Even better than your Grandma Ruthie's—but don't tell her I said so!"

Shawn laughed along with her dad. "Don't worry, Dad, I won't," she promised.

"So, what are you up to today?" Mr. Jordan asked.

Shawn shrugged. "Not sure," she admitted. "I might start my homework this afternoon. Or maybe I'll do it tomorrow."

"Get the homework out of the way," Mr. Jordan advised as he started rinsing the breakfast dishes.

"Well, of course you'd say that," Shawn retorted playfully. "Professor Jordan!" Shawn's dad was a professor at Brooklyn College, just like Mrs. Moore.

"Maybe so," Mr. Jordan said with a smile. "But it's always nicer to take care of chores early—then you're free to do whatever you want. For example, I want to work on my new book today. But first I'm going to make myself take down the Christmas decorations. Otherwise, I guarantee it, those decorations will be up for the rest of the month!"

Shawn laughed again. "Okay, okay," she gave in. "I'll definitely start my homework today."

"Great! I'll finish the dishes, baby girl."

"Thanks, Dad!" Shawn dried her hands on a dish towel and retreated to her bedroom, closing the door behind her. She glanced at her messenger bag full of heavy textbooks and shook her head. *It's way too early to start doing homework*, she thought. *The weekend just started!*

On Shawn's bedside table was the photo Mrs. Moore had given her the night before. She had looked at it for a long time before she'd finally fallen asleep. *I can't believe Mom's been gone for three years*, she thought, catching her breath. *I never thought life would go on. But it has...*

25

Suddenly, there was a tightness in Shawn's chest that she hadn't felt in many months. She took a deep breath. *Be calm*, she told herself. Sometimes, it frightened her—the overwhelming grief that snuck up on her when she thought about her mother.

Shawn glanced around the room, looking for something—anything—to distract her from feeling sad. She spotted the new easel her father had given her for Christmas. *I'll mess around with my paints*, Shawn decided. She rummaged through her art box and pulled out several tubes of blue paint: cobalt, cerulean, azure...Shawn loved the names of the colors. Shawn squeezed blobs of each color onto her shiny tin palette, plus large circles of white and black. With her favorite brush, Shawn swirled the colors together into dozens of shades of blue—light shades, dark shades, cool shades, warm shades. On the blank canvas before her, Shawn could picture the blues creating an image. Focusing on painting helped Shawn feel better for a little while...but she knew it was only a matter of time before the sadness would return.

chapter 3

The following Monday at school, Natasha dreaded telling her friends that she couldn't go on the ski trip. She wanted to wait until they were all together at lunchtime, but when she arrived at the Chef Girls' usual table, Peichi was already chatting away.

"So we were supposed to go shopping for new ski stuff on Sunday. But my mom wanted to look at baby things first. So we spent, like, *hours* and *hours* at Baby-Rama. I mean, the stuff was cute and all, but enough already! How many little booties can you look at before you go crazy? And then the worst part was that when we were finished, my mom was too tired to go to Sports Plus! Can you believe it?" Peichi complained.

The twins exchanged a glance and tried not to laugh. "That stinks, Peichi," Amanda said carefully. "But I'm sure your parents will take you shopping next weekend."

"Besides, you'd better get used to your mom and dad focusing on the baby," Molly said bluntly. "New parents always do that."

Peichi frowned at Molly.

"Nice, Molls," Amanda said, poking her sister. "Don't

27

worry, Peichi—your parents will always have time for you!" She cleared her throat, then changed the subject. "About the ski trip—I talked to Evan on the phone last night and got the inside scoop. We have to pick our bunks *right away*. Each bunk holds eight people, so we need to find three more girls to room with. Any ideas?"

"Um, Amanda," Natasha spoke up. "You'd better find *four* girls."

Everyone looked at Natasha, shocked.

"Huh? Aren't you coming on the trip?" asked Molly.

Natasha shrugged and tried to smile. "I don't think so. You know my parents..."

"I don't believe it! Why won't they let you go?" shrieked Amanda.

"My mom...she just thinks skiing is dangerous. And she doesn't like the thought of me going away without them for a long weekend." Natasha rolled her eyes.

"Oh, Natasha," Shawn said sympathetically.

"Don't worry, Natasha," Amanda said confidently. "We'll figure something out. You *have* to come on the ski trip! It wouldn't be the same without you! Hey, maybe our mom can talk to your mom. Do you think that would help?"

"Maybe," Natasha said.

"Yeah," Peichi added. "We could have a—what's it called? An intervention!" She started talking in a deep voice. "Mrs. Ross, we understand that you worry about

Natasha. But don't worry, we'll take very good care of her!" Everyone cracked up.

Natasha smiled at her friends—but inside, she thought, *They don't know my mom. It's not that easy.*

"Anyway," Amanda continued, "we still need three more people. How about Tessa Allen? She's so fun."

"And Elizabeth, of course," said Shawn. Elizabeth Derring had been on the cheerleading squad with Shawn until an ankle injury had forced her to quit. She and her aunt lived in an apartment on the top floor of Natasha's brownstone.

Amanda nodded and wrote down both names.

"Do you guys know Iris Perry?" asked Molly. "She's in my social studies and gym classes. She's cool."

"Yeah, she's the seventh-grade vice president," Amanda said. "I met her at a campaign meeting. She's really nice. Okay, let's ask Tessa, Elizabeth, and Iris today."

Before Amanda finished speaking, the bell rang. As the girls picked up their garbage, Molly leaned over to Natasha.

"Seriously, Natasha, don't worry," she said in a quiet voice. "We'll figure out a way for you to go on the trip!"

Natasha looked into Molly's bright green eyes and smiled at her friend. For the first time since she'd fought with her parents, Natasha felt that maybe, just maybe, everything would work out.

For the rest of the day, it seemed everyone in seventh grade was trying to figure out who would be in their bunks. Shawn was glad to have her bunk squared away—but when she went to the gym after school for cheerleading practice, she started to worry. *What if the cheerleaders want me to bunk with them?* she wondered. *It'll be really awkward because of the whole Angie mess.*

When Shawn had first joined the cheerleading squad, she and Angie Martinez had become close friends. But eventually, Shawn realized that Angie had a serious mean streak. She was rude to Shawn's other friends, especially Amanda. After Shawn had caught Angie stealing and vandalizing Elizabeth's new cheerleading shoes to keep her out of an important meet, Shawn had decided to end the friendship. Angie had not taken it well, and in the past few weeks, had focused her mean side on Shawn. So far, Shawn hadn't done anything about it. She hoped that Angie would eventually get sick of picking on her and leave her alone.

In the locker room, the seventh-grade cheerleaders were eagerly discussing the ski trip. But as Shawn walked over to her locker, their chatter stopped abruptly.

Weird, Shawn thought as she spun the dial on her combination lock. She cleared her throat. "What's up, everybody?" she asked.

There was an awkward silence, then Jenn spoke up. "We were, um, talking about the ski trip—figuring out our bunk and everything."

"Oh. Cool," Shawn said. There was another pause. *Who cares if they don't want me in their bunk? I'd rather bunk with the Chef Girls any day!*

"Um, Shawn. Do you want to bunk with us?" Jessica asked hesitantly.

Shawn found her voice. "Actually, I already said I'd bunk with some of my other friends," she said. "But thanks for asking."

"That's good," said a shrill voice. "Because our bunk is full."

Angie Martinez was standing in the doorway, her arms crossed in front of her and an icy smile on her face. From the smug tone in her voice, Shawn could tell how glad Angie was to be excluding Shawn.

"So it's really good that you found *somebody* to bunk with, Shawn," Angie continued. "There's no room for *you* in the cheerleader bunk."

Cut it out, Angie! Shawn thought fiercely as her face grew hot. *Why can't you leave me alone?* More than anything, Shawn wanted to tell Angie off. Instead, she took a deep breath and turned her back on Angie. *If I keep ignoring her, she'll eventually stop bugging me,* she told herself again. Though Shawn pretended Angie didn't bother her, she was painfully aware of Angie whispering about her for the rest of practice.

After practice, Shawn hurried back to the locker room and changed as quickly as she could. She wanted to get out of there before the rest of the squad started changing—and before Angie had another chance to embarrass her.

Shawn was almost finished changing when the other cheerleaders entered the locker room. "Good practice! See you later, guys," Shawn called over her shoulder as she left the locker room. As she walked out the door, Shawn thought she heard a couple cheerleaders start laughing. *Are they laughing at me?* Shawn wondered anxiously. Then she forced herself to calm down. *They're just laughing,* she told herself. *Don't be paranoid.*

Outside, dusk was falling, and the sky was cloudless and steely-gray. Shawn shivered and started to walk home quickly. On Monday nights, her father taught until six o'clock, but he was almost always home by six-thirty. *I'll get my homework done by the time Dad gets home. Then we can heat up the beef stew we made yesterday, and maybe watch a movie on TV. Or play Scrabble!*

When she got home, Shawn went straight to her room and pulled out her math book. She was concentrating on the third homework problem when the phone rang, jolting her out of her thoughts. Shawn jumped up from her desk and ran out to the kitchen to grab the cordless phone. *I*

hope Dad's not gonna be late tonight, she thought as she picked up the receiver.

"Hello?" Shawn answered.

Silence.

Then a soft click, and dial tone.

Wrong number, Shawn thought. She was about to put the receiver down when the phone rang in her hand.

"Hello?" Shawn answered after the first ring.

But again, no one was there.

Shawn stood in the empty apartment and looked around. Suddenly, it seemed too dark, too quiet. *I'll turn on the lights,* Shawn thought. *That will help.* Shawn went from room to room, turning on every light. Then she checked to make sure that the door was locked.

Better, Shawn thought, smiling at herself for feeling so freaked out by a couple of wrong numbers. She went back to her room. But as she sat down, the phone rang again.

"Hello?"

Click.

Shawn shivered. Suddenly she couldn't shake the feeling that she was being watched.

Brrrrring!
Brrrrring!
Brrrrring!

Shawn took a deep breath and answered the phone. This time, though, whoever was on the other end didn't hang up. Shawn almost thought she could hear someone breathing.

"What-what do you want?" Shawn asked, trying to keep her voice from quavering. "Why are you calling me?"

Click.

What am I gonna do? Shawn wondered, her heart pounding. It was only five-thirty—her father wouldn't be home for another hour.

The phone rang again.

"Forget it," Shawn said aloud, her voice echoing in the empty apartment. But the phone kept ringing, and ringing, and ringing.

Finally, after almost twenty rings, the phone stopped. The sudden silence in the apartment was overwhelming.

Shawn exhaled slowly—she hadn't even realized that she had been holding her breath.

Brrrrring!

Shawn grabbed the receiver. "*What? What* do you want?" Shawn cried.

"Shawn?" said Molly. "Is everything okay? What's wrong?"

At the sound of Molly's voice, Shawn almost started crying. "Molly, *ohmigosh*, I'm so glad it's you! Have you been trying to call me?"

"No, this is the first time. What's going on?"

"I've gotten, like, a million hang-up calls tonight," Shawn explained. "My dad's not home yet and I started to feel...scared." She laughed awkwardly. "That sounds pretty lame, doesn't it?"

"No way! That's really creepy," Molly said. "Who do you think it is?"

Shawn shrugged and walked over to the couch in the living room. She curled up under a cozy red afghan. "Who knows? Just some creep, probably."

There was a click on the line. "Hey, guys! What's up?" asked Amanda. Molly and Shawn filled her in on the hang-up calls. "That's totally bizarre," Amanda said. "Did you star-six-nine?"

"What's that?" Shawn asked.

"If somebody calls you, but you don't make it to the phone in time and they hang up, you can dial star-six-nine to get their phone number," Amanda explained. "I used to do it all the time—like, whenever I got home, just in case somebody had called, but didn't leave a message. Well, it turns out that it costs, like, seventy-five cents every time you do it! Mom and Dad were *not* happy when they got the phone bill!"

Everyone laughed, and Shawn started to relax.

"Are you still creeped out?" Molly asked. "Do you want to come over?"

Shawn glanced at the clock. "No, that's okay," she said. "Dad will be home soon. But, um, do you guys mind staying on the phone 'til he gets here?"

"No problem," Amanda replied. "Talking on phone is

practically my favorite thing to do!"

The girls laughed again, then Molly grew serious. "Shawn? Are you gonna tell your dad about the calls?"

Shawn thought for a moment. "I don't think so," she finally said. "It was probably just a one-time thing. And I don't want him to get all worried about me and make me stay at Mrs. Murphy's. I'm *way* too old for a baby-sitter. If it happens again, I'll tell him."

"Yeah," Amanda agreed. "It was probably nothing."

The twins and Shawn chatted for a few more minutes, then Shawn heard a key turn in the lock and her father's voice calling her name. "Dad's home," she said. "Gotta go. Thanks for staying on the phone with me."

"No big," Molly replied. "Walk to school tomorrow?"

"Of course! See you then."

Shawn hung up the phone as her father walked into the living room. "Hi there, baby girl," Mr. Jordan said with a grin. "How was your day? *Mmm*, I've been dreaming about that beef stew all afternoon! Hungry?"

"Starved!" Shawn exclaimed as she got up.

"Good!" said Mr. Jordan. "Let's go heat up that stew!"

As Shawn followed her father into the kitchen, she thought about how the entire apartment seemed to come alive as soon as he was home. The phone calls, the fear—all of that was forgotten now that he was home.

Almost.

The next morning, Shawn picked up the twins before school so the three of them could walk together. She was hoping they wouldn't bring up the hang-up calls. Fortunately, Amanda couldn't stop talking about the ski trip.

"So, Evan called me last night, and I asked him lots of questions about when he went on the ski trip last year," Amanda said. "Our bunk is all set—that is, if Natasha's parents let her go on the trip. I mean, I'm sure they will. But Evan told me that getting on the right bus is almost as important as the bunk."

"The right bus?" Molly asked blankly. "What does that mean?"

"*Well,*" Amanda explained importantly. "There are three buses and we have to sign up for the one we want to ride on. So, it's *really* important to sign up for the right one—the one with all your friends and the cool kids. Otherwise, you could get stuck on the loser bus."

Molly and Shawn stared at Amanda.

"What?" Amanda asked, confused.

"The 'loser' bus?" Molly asked, raising her eyebrows.

Amanda flushed. "You guys know what I mean! All

I'm saying is that we should sign up for the same bus. So we can sit together. It's a seven-hour drive, you know."

Shawn changed the subject. "Do you think Natasha's parents are going to the meeting about the ski trip tonight?"

"I think so," answered Molly. "Our mom called Mrs. Ross last night. Mom said, 'We want to get more information about the trip, too.'"

As the girls walked into the main hall of Windsor Middle School, they noticed a large crowd of students at the end of the corridor.

"What's going on down there?" Molly asked.

"Maybe they put up the bus lists!" Amanda said excitedly.

"Down at the end of the hall? I don't think so," Shawn replied. "Maybe there was a fight or something."

The girls walked down the hall, toward the crowd. Suddenly, Shawn stopped and frowned. "It looks like they're in front of my locker."

As Shawn began to walk faster, the twins exchanged a glance. They were doing the "twin thing" again, thinking, *Why are there so many people in front of Shawn's locker?*

Shawn pushed her way through the crowd, then gasped when she saw her locker. It was smeared with bright red paint, the dripping letters reading *SHAWN JORDAN IS A LOSER!*

The crowd grew quiet as everyone stared at Shawn. Amanda quickly put her arm around her friend. "Let's get out of here," she murmured. The twins led Shawn down the hall and into the main office.

Miss Hinkle, the secretary, looked up when they entered. "Good morning, girls!" she sang out cheerfully.

Away from the staring eyes of the crowd, Shawn burst into tears.

"Oh my goodness, oh, dear, what's the matter?" Miss Hinkle asked, coming out from behind her desk with a box of tissues.

"Shawn's locker is covered in graffiti!" Molly said angrily. "Big red letters that say 'Shawn Jordan is a loser!'"

Miss Hinkle shook her head. "Dreadful. Just dreadful." She patted Shawn on the shoulder and went to the phone. "Mrs. Wagner? Do you have a moment? There seems to have been some vandalism to a student's locker. She's here now...yes, very upset...thank you." Miss Hinkle hung up the phone and turned to Shawn with a sympathetic smile. "Principal Wagner will be right out," she said kindly.

A few minutes later, Principal Wagner appeared. "Hello, Shawn," she said. "Why don't you come in to my office. Molly and Amanda, you can come, too."

Shawn and the twins stood automatically and followed Principal Wagner.

Molly looked at Amanda as if to say, *How did she know our names?* Amanda just shrugged, as if to say, *Principal Wagner is one of those people who knows* everything!

Principal Wagner gestured to two chairs in front of her desk, then pulled up a third. As Molly, Amanda, and Shawn sat, Principal Wagner asked, "What happened?"

Shawn took a deep breath. "When we got to school, we saw this big crowd in front of my locker," she began. "We thought maybe there had been a fight. But when we got closer, I saw that there was writing on my locker. It said, 'Shawn Jordan is a loser!'" Shawn looked at the floor. In the distance, the girls heard the bell for homeroom ring.

"I see," Principal Wagner said seriously. "So the graffiti was already there when you got to school. Do you have any idea who might have done this?"

Shawn looked up. "No," she said. "I have no idea."

Principal Wagner looked at Shawn for a moment, then nodded her head. "All right. We'll have the janitor remove the paint at once. Shawn, if anything like this happens again, I want you to come tell me right away. Okay?"

"Thanks, Principal Wagner," Shawn said, trying to smile.

"I'll have Miss Hinkle write you passes to go to homeroom," Principal Wagner said. She walked Shawn, Molly, and Amanda to the door.

Out in the hall, Amanda turned to Shawn. "Why didn't you tell her about Angie?"

Shawn shrugged. "There's no proof it was Angie. All that would happen is Principal Wagner would talk to Angie and tell her not to do it again—if she *did* do it. If I tell on Angie, she'll just hate me even more."

"But Shawn—" Molly began.

"Anyway, I don't care," Shawn interrupted, her voice growing louder. "The janitor will fix my locker. We can forget about it. See you guys at lunch, okay?" Shawn gave the twins a little wave and hurried off to homeroom.

The twins exchanged a glance.

"Whoa. Why's she mad at us?" Amanda asked quietly.

"She's not," Molly replied. "She's upset and she's trying to pretend it never happened."

"Well, that's not gonna be easy," Amanda said darkly. "*Everyone* is going to be talking about this."

"What I want to know is how Principal Wagner knew our names," Molly said thoughtfully.

"I think she knows *everything*," Amanda replied. "Did you see the way she looked at Shawn when Shawn said she didn't know who did the graffiti? It was like she could tell Shawn wasn't being totally honest. I still think Shawn should have told her about Angie."

"Well, it's Shawn's choice," Molly replied. "I just hope Angie gets tired of picking on her soon."

"Me, too," said Amanda. "But I don't think she will."

Mooretimes2: hey chef grrrlzzz! s'up?

BrooklynNatasha: not much. Just chillin, listening 2 some CDs.

Qtpie490: kewl. I'm e-mailing grandma ruthie.

Mooretimes2: are anybody's parents back yet?

Happyface: nope.

Qtpie490: ditto.

BrooklynNatasha: same here.

Mooretimes2: guess the ski trip meeting is still going on. It's a long one! Hey, this is Amanda. After school, the bus lists were posted outside the main office! I signed us all up for Bus #1.

Happyface: sweet! Thx.

BrooklynNatasha: even me?

Mooretimes2: of course! U are so coming on this trip.

BrooklynNatasha: I hope so!!! Oh hang on—I think my parents r home. Eeeeek! I'm totally nervous. What if they say no again?

Mooretimes2: they won't! we'll keep our fingers crossed.

Happyface: me 2.

Qtpie490: me 3!

BrooklynNatasha: u guys are seriously the best. See u tomorrow @ school.

Natasha quickly logged off the Internet and went downstairs. Her parents were in the kitchen, making tea and talking quietly. "Hey, Mom and Dad," Natasha began. "Um, how was the meeting?"

"It was very...informative," Mrs. Ross said, adding some sugar to her peppermint tea. "Your father and I haven't reached a decision yet."

"That's okay," Natasha said. "I didn't want to bug you guys about it. It just seemed like a long meeting."

Mr. Ross nodded. "It was. But that's because the teachers were giving us so much information."

"I must say, Principal Wagner and Mr. Degregorio have done an excellent job planning the trip," Mrs. Ross said thoughtfully. Then she turned to Natasha. "Daddy and I will discuss everything tonight, sweetheart," she said. "We'll give you an answer tomorrow."

"Okay," Natasha said. She kissed her mother on the cheek, then gave her father a hug. "Good night."

"Good night, Natasha," replied her parents.

As Natasha got ready for bed, she thought, *Wow! It sounds like the meeting went really well! Mom definitely seems open to the idea. Maybe Dad can convince her. Maybe he's convincing her right now! Oh, I hope I get to go. I hope, I hope, I hope...*

The next morning, Natasha woke before her alarm clock rang. It took her a minute to realize why she felt so anxious—and then she remembered. Today, her parents would tell her if she could go on the ski trip.

Natasha hurried downstairs to see if her parents were up. Her father was making coffee. "Good morning, princess," he said, his eyes twinkling.

"Morning, Dad," replied Natasha. "Where's Mom?"

"She's still upstairs," Mr. Ross said. "We were up pretty late last night. We did a lot of talking..." He grinned at Natasha as he took a sip of his coffee.

"And?" Natasha asked, biting her lip nervously.

"You can go!" Mrs. Ross said as she walked into the kitchen. She looked older than usual—her eyes were tired and she wasn't wearing any makeup—but a smile spread across her face.

"*Really? Really?!*" Natasha squealed. "Oh, thank you! Oh, this is fantastic! I can't wait to tell the Chef Girls!"

"There are two conditions, though," Mrs. Ross said. "You've got to be completely prepared for your bat mitzvah *before* the trip. And Daddy and I are going to be chaperones. We both feel more comfortable with you going away if we're nearby."

"Okay," Natasha said quickly. "That's fine. Oh, I can't wait! Thanks so much, Mom and Dad!"

Natasha couldn't stop smiling as she got ready for school. She decided to wear her favorite outfit—a purple

44

corduroy skirt with a white sweater—and pulled her hair back with hand-painted barrettes Shawn had made for her birthday. Fifteen minutes later, she met Elizabeth on the front walk of the house.

"Guess what?" Natasha shrieked. "I can go on the trip!"

Elizabeth jumped up and down and gave Natasha a hug. *Ohmigosh!* That's so awesome!" she squealed. "How'd you convince your parents?"

"Actually, it was the informational meeting last night that convinced them," Natasha explained. "And they decided they would chaperone, too."

Elizabeth frowned and put her hand on Natasha's arm. "Yuck," she said. "That's too bad."

"Wh-what do you mean?" Natasha asked. Then her eyes grew wide. "You're so right. It's totally lame for my *parents* to come on the trip, isn't it?"

Elizabeth shrugged and tried to make Natasha feel better. "Look at the bright side—at least you get to go!" she said cheerfully. "It'll be okay."

"No—it's going to be totally embarrassing!" Natasha moaned. "My parents aren't exactly cool. What if they try to spend, like, the entire trip with me? What if they're really strict with everybody?"

"Don't worry so much, Natasha," replied Elizabeth. "You're coming on the trip! Yay!"

Natasha returned Elizabeth's smile, but she felt a lot less excited than she had a few minutes ago.

After school, Natasha and Molly went to a meeting for the school newspaper, the *Post*. They found two seats together near the window and chatted while they waited for Liza Pederson, the editor, to start the meeting.

"Hey, Molly, what's up? Hi, Natasha." Justin McElroy dropped his backpack on the seat in front of Molly and sat down.

"Not much, Justin. What's up with you?"

Justin shrugged. "Same old, same old. School, *Post*, all that stuff. Are you going out for softball again?"

Molly nodded. "Definitely. I had a blast last year!"

"And you were one of the best players on the team," Justin said, his brown eyes lighting up. "We should do a profile on you for the *Post*. Molly Moore, softball star!"

Molly could tell that Natasha was trying not to laugh. Justin sounded so *goofy*—it was a little annoying. Annoying, but also flattering.

When Molly had first found out that Justin liked her as more than a friend, she'd been shocked—and worried. Amanda had been crushing on Justin for more than a year! Molly was afraid that Amanda would never forgive her, even though Molly hadn't meant for Justin to start liking her. It had been difficult for Amanda to deal with the fact that her crush liked her sister, but, over time,

Amanda had realized that she and Justin didn't have that much in common. She was finally over him. But Molly's feelings were mixed. She wasn't sure if she liked Justin or not—and wasn't sure how to act around him.

Fortunately, Natasha jumped into the conversation. "Justin, do you ski?" she asked.

"Oh, yeah," Justin said excitedly. "My whole family goes skiing every winter."

"I've never been," Natasha admitted.

"You'll love it! I mean, everyone in my family is a ski nut, but you can still have a great time on the bunny slopes," Justin said.

"Bunny slopes?"

"Yeah, those are little hills for beginners. Nice and easy. My parents are such ski fanatics that as soon as they found out about the trip, they volunteered to chaperone."

"*Really?*" Natasha exclaimed. "My parents are chaperoning, too! But I don't think they're that crazy about skiing."

Justin smiled his slow, easy grin. "Bet they will be after the trip!"

Just then, Liza called the meeting to order. As she began discussing feature articles for the next issue of the *Post*, Natasha couldn't help smiling. *Justin's cool...if his parents are chaperoning, it can't be totally lame for my mom and dad to come on the trip!*

The next two weeks were busy for all of the Chef Girls as they prepared for the trip. Between school and activities, Dish, and shopping for ski gear, it almost seemed like the trip sneaked up on them. Natasha was extra-busy as she prepared for her bat mitzvah. In a way, though, she was relieved to study hard. Being completely ready for her bat mitzvah made her feel a little less nervous.

The night before the trip, Natasha sat on her parents' bed, watching her mom and dad pack their suitcases. *Mom is, like, crazy-organized,* Natasha thought with a smile as she watched her mother pack outfits for each day of the trip, carefully checking off a list.

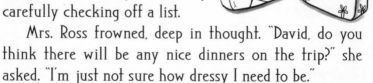

Mrs. Ross frowned, deep in thought. "David, do you think there will be any nice dinners on the trip?" she asked. "I'm just not sure how dressy I need to be."

"It's gonna be really casual, Mom," Natasha said quickly. "It's a cabin out in the woods and a bunch of seventh-graders. You should probably bring a lot of jeans and pants and warm sweaters. Like, wooly sweaters, not the pretty ones you have with the beads."

"This is what I'm bringing," Mr. Ross said proudly, emptying a shopping bag onto the bed. Out fell five brand-new flannel button-down shirts.

"Oh, David," laughed Mrs. Ross. "You'll look just like a lumberjack!"

"I like them, Dad," Natasha spoke up as she pulled one on. "They're so cozy!"

After Mrs. Ross filled her large suitcase, she pulled out a medium-sized one and began packing more sweaters and fleecy nightgowns.

"Um, Mom?" Natasha asked. "Do you think...do you think that might be too much stuff? It's only a few days."

"Sweetheart, I just want to make sure I have the right outfits," she replied. "By the way, how is *your* packing going? Would you like some help?"

"That's okay, I'm already done," replied Natasha, thinking of the ski pants, parka, three pairs of jeans, two sweatshirts, and two sweaters she had packed in a small duffel bag.

Just then, the phone rang.

"I'll get it!" Natasha scrambled over the bed and grabbed the cordless phone on her parents' nightstand.

"Natasha! Shoes off the bed!" Mrs. Ross exclaimed.

Making a face, Natasha swung her feet over the side of the bed. "Hello?"

"Hello, is Natasha there?" asked a boy's voice.

"This is Natasha."

49

"Oh, hey, Natasha! It's Connor."

"Hi." Natasha walked into the hallway. "What's up?"

"Oh, nothin'. Um, are you all packed for the trip?"

"Yes. How about you?"

"Um. I'm mostly packed. You know..." Connor cleared his throat. "I'm, uh, really excited."

"So am I!"

"Yeah. Anyway, I was, uh, wondering what time we have to be at school tomorrow."

"Oh, six a.m.," Natasha replied. Connor groaned, and she laughed. "I know. It's so *early*."

"Seriously! I mean, why do we have to leave at the crack of dawn? It's not like the slopes are going anywhere!"

Natasha laughed again.

"Anyway, uh, see you tomorrow?" Connor said.

"Okay. Bye, Connor."

"Who was that, Natasha?" Mrs. Ross asked from the bedroom.

"Oh, just this guy from school, Connor," Natasha answered, still smiling.

Her father caught her eye and smiled back. "Oh, really? Who is this Connor? Have I met him before?"

"Oh, *Dad*," Natasha said, rolling her eyes. "He just wanted to know what time we have to be at school tomorrow."

"Oh, really?" asked Mr. Ross, continuing to tease her.

"Well, why didn't he call one of his buddies to find out?"

Natasha opened her mouth, then closed it. *That's a good question*, she thought. *Why didn't he call Omar or Justin? Unless...no...*

She looked up to see both of her parents watching her. "Um, I dunno," Natasha answered, shrugging. "I'm going to get ready for bed now. Night!"

As Natasha washed her face, she smiled at herself in the mirror. *Maybe Connor was calling just to talk to me!*

The next morning dawned pink and cold, the bright red sun blazing on the horizon. At the Moores' house, Amanda sat straight up in bed as soon as the alarm rang. "Ski trip day!" she shrieked. "Wake up, Molls! Wake up!" Amanda happily tossed her pillow across the room, where it landed on Molly's head.

"*Argh!* Wh-*what?*" Molly, startled by the pillow, sat up in bed. She blinked sleepily, then saw Amanda's grinning face hovering over her. "*Ugh*...Manda, you're such a pain in the morning," Molly mumbled, pulling the puffy comforter over her head.

Amanda promptly pulled it off. "Up, up, up," she sang. "Come on, Molls! It's already after five! We have to leave in thirty minutes! I'm gonna brush my teeth and you better be getting dressed by the time I get out of the bathroom!"

There was a soft knock, and Mom came in the door, dressed in sweatpants and a fleecy sweatshirt. "Morning, girls," she said with a smile. "There are pancakes and hot chocolate downstairs. I want you to eat a good breakfast before we leave, okay?"

"*Mmm*, pancakes," Molly said, stretching.

"I knew that would get you up!" Amanda giggled as she skipped into the bathroom. "Molly, aren't you excited? It's finally here—the class ski trip!"

"I am excited—or I will be, in an hour or two," said Molly with a yawn. "Once I wake up a little!"

Thirty minutes later, when the twins arrived at Windsor Middle School, Molly was wide awake—and just as excited as Amanda. Three coach buses were lined up in front of the school, and dozens of students and parents were milling about, checking in with the bus monitors, dropping off luggage, and saying good-bye. The twins had said good-bye to Dad at home since Matthew was still asleep, and Mom didn't want to leave him by himself.

"Molly! Amanda! Over here!"

The twins saw Peichi standing with her parents near

Bus #1, waving wildly. "I couldn't wait to come over to the school so we got here *really* early! The buses weren't even here yet! Fortunately, Mr. D. was and he let us wait inside the school. I felt so silly, but I'm just so psyched!"

The twins laughed along with Mr. and Mrs. Cheng. "Don't burn off all that energy too soon, Peichi," cautioned Mrs. Cheng.

"Hey, Chef Girls!" Shawn called out as she hurried over to Peichi and the twins, her father following behind her, carrying her suitcase.

As the girls and their parents greeted one another, Shawn glanced around. "Where's Natasha?" she asked. "Is she here yet?"

Peichi nodded at the check-in tables. "The Rosses got here right after we did. They're the bus monitors for our bus, and they're checking in kids over there. See? I think Natasha is helping."

"So, Peichi," said Mr. Jordan. "You seem to know the drill. What do we do now?"

"First, you check in with your bus monitor," Peichi said. "Then you drop off your luggage. There are different spots for each bus. But we're on the same bus together! Yay! It's gonna rock! Come on, I'm already checked in, but I'll come with you guys."

"And we'll go say hi to the Rosses," Mom said.

Everyone followed Peichi to the check-in table for Bus #1. As soon as Natasha saw her friends, she broke away from her parents and hurried over to them.

"Hey! Can you believe my parents are our bus monitors? Totally lame!" Natasha whispered to the Chef Girls. "They already asked me if I wanted to sit with them, but I said, 'No way, I'm sitting with my friends!' I'm really glad that they aren't going to be our bunk chaperones. We got Mrs. Lopez instead."

"She's our homeroom teacher!" exclaimed Amanda and Molly.

Amanda giggled. "I hope we don't see her in her pajamas or—"

"Or with cold cream all over her face!" shrieked Molly.

Mrs. Ross greeted the girls warmly as Mr. Ross checked their names off the list. But when Shawn got to the front of the line, he frowned. "James, Jerrod, Kingston...Shawn, you're not on this list."

"That's not possible. I wrote *everybody's* name down," Amanda replied.

Mr. Ross shook his head and showed the girls the list.

"Then which bus am I on?" Shawn asked, puzzled.

"You're on *our* bus," Amanda said firmly. "Come on, let's go talk to Mrs. Lopez." She took Shawn by the arm and hurried off to find Mrs. Lopez, who was standing near the luggage, looking frazzled.

"Graham! Richard! Knock it off!" Mrs. Lopez yelled at two boys who were making a tower of suitcases. Then she turned to Amanda and Shawn. "Yes, girls, what is it?"

"Mrs. Lopez, there's a mix-up with the buses," Amanda

explained quickly. "Shawn is supposed to be on Bus #1. But her name isn't on the list."

Mrs. Lopez frowned, then pulled the sign-up sheets out of a folder. Amanda grabbed the sheet for Bus #1. "Look!" she cried. "Here's where I wrote Shawn's name. But someone crossed it off!"

Amanda and Shawn glanced at the other sign-up sheets. At the bottom of the sheet for Bus #3, someone had scrawled *SHAWN JORDAN* in messy handwriting.

"Oh, no!" Shawn exclaimed. "Angie is on Bus #3. And the other cheerleaders are, too!"

"Mrs. Lopez, this is wrong," Amanda insisted. "Shawn is supposed to be on Bus #1, not Bus #3."

Mrs. Lopez glanced at the list, then shook her head. "I'm sorry, girls, but the buses are full. Shawn has to ride on Bus #3. Richard! I'm not going to say it again!"

"But—" Shawn began. "But all of my friends are on Bus #1."

"Shawn, I'm sorry, but we need to leave in fifteen minutes. You can make a new friend on Bus #3." With that, Mrs. Lopez hurried off to find Mr. Degregorio.

"This stinks!" Amanda said angrily. "Why would someone cross off your name? That's awful!"

Shawn tried to smile. "Well, at least we're in the same bunk together. That's more important, right?"

"Of course!" replied Amanda, secretly relieved that Shawn was trying to look on the bright side.

Wheeeeeeeet!

Mr. Degregorio stood at the top of the steps, blowing his silver whistle. Instantly, everyone stopped talking and turned to face him.

"Ladies and gentlemen! In fifteen short minutes, we will be departing for Chestnut Hill Farm, Vermont! In the next five minutes, you need to say good-bye to your parents and board your bus. We'll be doing roll call on each bus. Okay?"

"Okay!" shouted the entire seventh-grade class.

Amanda and Shawn hurried over to where their parents were standing with the other Chef Girls. There was barely time to explain to them that Shawn had to ride on Bus #3. Mr. Jordan wrapped Shawn in a bear hug and kissed her. "Have a great time, baby," he whispered into her hair. "I love you."

"Love you, too, Dad," Shawn whispered back. She always hated saying good-bye to her father, and the thought of spending the next seven hours on a bus with Angie, away from all of her friends, didn't make it any easier.

Shawn and her father dropped off her luggage in the pile for Bus #3, then she waved good-bye to her friends and boarded the bus. *I'm glad I brought my Discman and headphones,* Shawn thought. *And my magazines. If nobody wants to talk to me, that's fine.* Shawn settled into a seat next to a window in the middle of the bus, which was soon filled with loud, laughing kids.

When Angie got on the bus, snapping her gum, her cold brown eyes scanned the seats. She didn't even try to hide a nasty smile when she saw Shawn sitting all by herself.

"Come on, ladies!" Angie called over her shoulder in an imitation of Coach Carson, the head of the cheerleading squad. The rest of the seventh-grade cheerleaders giggled as they followed Angie down the aisle to the back of the bus. Jenn and Jessica smiled weakly at Shawn, and Shawn forced herself to grin back.

"Can I sit here?"

Shawn looked up to see Grace Daniels, a shy seventh-grader with pale blonde hair, standing next to her seat. "Of course," Shawn replied with a smile. *Grace always seems really nice*, Shawn thought. *Maybe the ride won't be so bad after all.*

Mr. Yamamoto, a science teacher, began to call roll. Suddenly, Angie popped out of her seat. "I packed my Discman in the wrong bag!" she called out as she pushed her way down the aisle. "I'll be right back!"

Mr. Yamamoto sighed. "Hurry up, Angie. And spit out that gum, too."

A few minutes later, Angie boarded the bus again. "Here I am! We can leave now," she shrieked. It was all Shawn could do to keep from rolling her eyes right at Angie. *It's so annoying when Angie is crazy-hyper like this,* Shawn thought. *I hope she settles down once we get moving.*

But Angie was more hyper than Shawn had ever seen her. Even though Angie was sitting at the very back of the bus, Shawn could hear her shrill laugh constantly. Shawn turned to Grace to start a conversation, but Grace was already intently reading a thick book. Shawn sighed as she put on her headphones. *This is going to be a long, boring ride,* she thought. *At least my music will drown out Angie's obnoxious laugh.*

On Bus #1, Molly, Amanda, Peichi, and Natasha found four seats next to one another.

"Poor Shawn," Natasha said quietly. "I can't believe she has to ride on Angie's bus."

"I know," Molly replied. "It's not gonna be the same without her."

"Too bad we couldn't have traded Omar for Shawn," Peichi joked as Omar, Connor, and Justin noisily boarded the bus.

Omar spotted the Chef Girls and made his way down the aisle toward where they were sitting. "Hello, la-a-dies!" he called out in his booming voice. "If you need anything, I'm your man." Omar unzipped his backpack to show the girls several bags of chips, bottles of sports drinks, CDs, and a huge roll of duct tape.

"What's that for?" Peichi asked, pointing at the duct tape.

Omar smiled mischievously. "You can do anything with duct tape. You'll see," he said, then continued down the aisle until he reached the very back of the bus.

As the bus started up, Amanda grabbed Molly's arm. "Here we go!" she squealed. Around them, all the students cheered.

Mr. Degregorio stood in the aisle at the front of the bus, where he was sitting across from Mr. and Mrs. Ross. "Okay, okay, people," he said with a smile. "It's fine to talk with your neighbor, but let's try to keep the noise down to a dull roar."

Peichi turned around in her seat. "I want to see what Omar's up to with that duct tape," she said. "*Ohmigosh!* He's making pictures on the windows with it! And writing stuff!"

Omar looked up and caught Peichi's eye. He yanked off a long piece of tape, then held the roll up in the air like he was going to throw it.

"Omar, don't!" Peichi called back to him.

Omar grinned, then rolled the duct tape down the aisle. Peichi reached over and picked it up.

"Well, what should we do with this?"

"I know!" Molly said. "I'm gonna write 'Chef Girls Rule!' on our window!"

"And I'll write 'Dish 4-Eva!' " Natasha said, taking the tape from Molly.

The roll of duct tape was passed throughout the whole bus, and soon nearly every window was covered with kids' names, funny sayings, and duct-tape pictures.

Suddenly, loud rap music blasted through the bus, and Omar was standing in the aisle, dancing along. The entire bus started laughing.

"Whoa!" yelled Omar as the bus turned a corner and he pitched into the seats on his left. Everyone cracked up.

"Mr. Kazdan, please take your seat," Mr. Degregorio called out from the front of the bus.

"Sure thing, Teach," Omar called back. He quickly sat down and started waving his hands around in the air. "Okay if I do a little seat-dancing, Mr. D.?"

Mr. D. couldn't help smiling. "Yes, Omar, that should be fine."

Natasha leaned forward to Molly and Amanda. "Omar is totally insane! This is gonna be the party bus!"

"It is," Molly agreed. "Get ready for a crazy ride!"

Meanwhile, further down the highway, Shawn couldn't wait for the trip to be over. She slept for a little while, though even in her dreams she thought she could hear Angie's nasty laugh. Shawn woke with a start and shook her head. *Let it go*, Shawn thought to herself. *Don't let Angie ruin this trip for you. Oh, I can't wait to get there. I can't wait to be with the Chef Girls again!*

Several hours later, the buses turned off the highway onto a narrow, two-lane country road. Enormous pine trees lined the road and, in the distance, Shawn could see snow-covered mountains reaching up to the sky. She felt a shiver of excitement and turned to Grace. "Look! Look how beautiful that is!"

Grace looked up from her book and smiled. "It is! Before we moved to Brooklyn, my mom and I lived in Maine," she said. "Even though we've been in Brooklyn for four years, pine trees always make me think of home."

"I've always lived in Brooklyn," Shawn said with a laugh. "To me, brownstones are home."

A few minutes later, a kid near the front of the bus yelled, "Check out that sign—'Chestnut Hill Farm!'" Everyone on the bus screamed and cheered.

Soon, the buses pulled up in front of a large cabin. Mr. Yamamoto stood in the front of the bus. "Listen up," he said sternly. "We're all going into the lodge for bunk assignments. Then you'll come back here to get your luggage and go to your cabins to settle in. We'll meet back in the lodge at five o'clock."

The students scrambled off the bus and filed into the front room of the cool old lodge, which was filled with comfortable couches and armchairs, old books, and board games. Shawn searched through the crowd until she saw her friends.

"Molly! Amanda! *Argh!* I'm so glad we're finally here!" Shawn cried. "I missed you guys."

"Poor Shawn," Natasha said. "Were you totally bored?"

Shawn nodded. "Yeah. But I sat next to Grace Daniels, who's really nice."

"Well, the important thing is that we're all together now," Peichi announced. "Now the fun can really start!"

Elizabeth ran up to the girls. "Hey, everybody! I just checked the bunk assignments—we're in Cabin Four. I can't wait to see it! Let's get our luggage and go!"

Elizabeth led the way over to the piles of suitcases and bags, followed by Amanda, Molly, Peichi, Natasha, Tessa, and Iris. Shawn found her suitcase in the pile of bags for Bus #3 and then quickly joined her friends. Together, they followed signs leading to the cabins. The snow on the path crunched beneath their shoes.

"My toes are cold! I can't wait to change into my boots!" Peichi said, hopping around in her sneakers. Her breath made tiny puffs of steam in the chilly air.

Iris inhaled deeply. "It smells so *good* here!" she exclaimed. "The pine trees...the snow...the air smells, like, so *clean*. I love it!"

"And it's so quiet," Amanda added. The girls stopped and listened. There were no cars, no buses, no sirens—just a peaceful stillness that surrounded them.

"Look! There it is!" Molly interrupted, pointing toward a log cabin with a sign in front of it that read *CABIN #4* in green paint.

"I love it! It looks so old-fashioned!" Amanda raved. The wooden cabin was a large room with eight single beds; each bed was covered with a thick patchwork quilt in a rainbow of colors. A small staircase in one corner of the room led up to a loft. There was an old, spotted mirror in the other corner, and a tiny bathroom behind a door. Three exposed lightbulbs hung from the ceiling, and a small window on each wall let in bright light from the reflection of the snow.

"That loft must be where Mrs. Lopez will sleep," Natasha said thoughtfully. *I'm so glad Mom's not chaperoning our bunk!*

"Okay," Molly said, taking charge. "Let's pick our beds and start unpacking."

The girls scrambled for the bunks, each one picking

the quilt she thought was prettiest. Then they started unpacking.

Molly shook her head. "Amanda, I still can't believe you brought two suitcases for only five days," she said as she dragged one of Amanda's bags over to her chest. "What's in here, anyway—rocks?"

"Ha, ha, ha," Amanda rolled her eyes playfully. "I'm used to bringing enough clothes for both of us, since *you* under-pack anytime we go anywhere!"

"*Ewww!*" squealed Shawn.

"What's wrong, Shawn?" Elizabeth asked.

"The zipper on my suitcase! It's all stuck together with chewed gum! Yuck! This is so sick!" Shawn jumped up and ran over to the tiny sink, where she tried to wash the sticky gum off her hand.

"*Ohmigosh!* Shawn, that's awful!" Amanda exclaimed. She and Molly hurried over to the suitcase. The two zipper pulls were covered with a glob of pink gum that was even stuck into the zipper's teeth.

"We'll get it off," Molly said quickly, pulling a tissue out of her pocket. But the tissue just stuck to the gum, making it worse.

"Oh! I know! Rubbing alcohol!" Amanda exclaimed. "I brought it to sterilize my earrings. But it also works on gum." It took about twenty minutes, but finally Amanda was able to get all of the gum off the zipper.

"Poor Shawn," Tessa said. "You've been having the worst luck lately."

"Yeah," Shawn said. She didn't say what she was thinking: *This is more than just bad luck.*

Molly cleared her throat and smiled brightly. "Well, I think that's all done with now. From here on, we're just going to have fun, fun, *fun!*"

Shawn smiled gratefully at Molly and thought, *I hope she's right, right, right.*

Half an hour later, the girls had finished unpacking and were making their way over to the lodge for the five o'clock meeting. As they walked, Shawn and the twins fell toward the back of the group.

"I know things have been lousy lately, Shawn," Molly began. "First those scary phone calls, then your locker, and getting stuck on Angie's bus, and now your suitcase. But we're gonna watch your back! You've got your best girls with you." At the same time, Amanda and Molly linked arms with Shawn.

"I know. You guys are the best," Shawn said simply. But there was still an edge of worry in her voice.

The girls passed some of the other cabins on their way to the lodge. Suddenly, Shawn heard Angie's cackling laugh and saw her standing in the doorway of Cabin

Nineteen with some of the other cheerleaders. Angie stared at Shawn, and started whispering to the cheerleaders, who dissolved into giggles. Then, looking right at Shawn, Angie blew an enormous bubble. The other cheerleaders laughed like it was the most hysterical thing ever.

Shawn felt Amanda stiffen on her left. "*Ooh!* She is so *evil*!" Amanda hissed.

"Ignore it," Shawn said quietly. She looked straight ahead and tried to make herself walk slowly, as if Angie wasn't bothering her at all.

As soon as they were out of Angie's sight, Amanda turned to Shawn. "Shawn, *tell* someone!" Amanda exclaimed. "This is horrible! Angie has *got* to stop picking on you like this!"

But Shawn just shook her head and looked down at the ground.

"Well," Molly said grimly. "At least we know who did it."

"Yeah, right," Amanda snorted. "Like there was any doubt."

In the lodge, Mr. Degregorio stood in the middle of the rec room and blew his whistle. Everyone grew quiet.

"Welcome to Chestnut Hill Farm, everyone! To begin, I'd like to introduce Mr. and Mrs. Hudson, who own this farm. They run it year-round and open it to campers during the summer, and to special tours, like us, during the winter. What they say goes, okay?"

Mr. and Mrs. Hudson, a kindly-looking couple in their late fifties, waved and smiled at the students.

"Now, let me introduce our chaperones. You all know Mrs. Lopez, Mr. Yamamoto, Mr. Nielsen, Ms. Francis, Miss Kwan, Mr. Bainbridge, and Mrs. Danu from school. Our parent chaperones are Detective and Mrs. McElroy, Mr. and Mrs. Ross, Mr. and Mrs. Portchoy, Mr. Hernandez, Mrs. Polkington, and Mr. and Mrs. Ting. One chaperone will stay in each bunk. Like I said before, whatever they say, goes. Right?"

"Right!" chorused the students.

"Under no circumstances should boys go into the girls' cabins, or vice versa. If you get caught, you will be sent home immediately." Mr. Degregorio gestured to some charts that were propped up on one of the walls. "These are the Chore Charts. I'll put a new one up each morning. They tell you which activities you have when. Generally, the work activities, like farming and cleaning, are in the morning, and the afternoons are for free time—you can ski or snowboard, or hang out in your cabin, or here in the lodge. Two or more bunks will be grouped together for each chore. Now I'm going to turn the floor over to Mr. Hudson so that he can go over the rules."

Mr. Hudson smiled at the students and cleared his throat. "Mrs. Hudson and I want to welcome all of you to

Chestnut Hill Farm," he began. "We don't have a lot of rules here, but the ones we do have are real important. There are four slopes along our mountain—bunny slopes for beginners, intermediate slopes, and advanced slopes. Then there's the Five Point slope. We call it Five Point because it's the tallest mountain of the five big ones in the range. You're only allowed to ski that one if you're over eighteen. Okay?"

"Okay!" chorused the students, though some of the more athletic kids groaned.

"It's a mean slope—lots of boulders, trees, and sudden turns. You've got to be a pro to handle it. Every year, two or three fools wipe out—and the results aren't pretty."

Mr. Hudson paused for a moment and glanced at his wife. She stood and smiled. "Lights out is at ten every night. Breakfast is served every morning at eight a.m.— don't be late or you'll miss it! Lunch is at one o'clock, and dinner is at six. And, since it's about five-thirty now, let's all get ready for dinner!"

The Hudsons led the way through large double doors on the left side of the room, which opened into an enormous dining room filled with long, wooden tables and benches.

"*Mmm*, that smells delicious!" Molly said. "I wonder what they're serving tonight."

"I can't wait for our turn in the kitchen," Amanda commented. "We're gonna blow everyone away!"

"I can't wait to hit the slopes," Peichi said. "Wait 'til you guys see my new ski suit! It's aqua-blue with fuchsia trim! I love it so much! As soon as I saw it, I knew that it was *perfect* and I totally wanted it! Hey, look! They're bringing in the food!"

Swinging double doors between the dining room and the kitchen burst open, and six waiters and waitresses began carrying in enormous trays heaped with platters of steaming food. A young woman stopped at the Chef Girls' table, smiling as she set down the heavy tray.

"*Phew!* I'm always a little worried I won't make it to the table," she joked, making everyone at the table chuckle. "My name is Vicky, and I'm a ski instructor here. And, as you can see, a waitress, too. We've got a great meal for you tonight. We call this dish Snowshoe Chicken—it's chicken breasts with a rich maple-mustard sauce. For sides, we have mashed potatoes and gravy, glazed carrots, and green salad. There's milk and soda and water on that table by the wall. But, whatever you do, make sure you save room for dessert!" Vicky winked at the girls, then hurried back to the kitchen.

"Save room for dessert? Not a problem," joked Amanda. Her friends laughed—Amanda had a serious sweet tooth!

"Wow, this chicken is so juicy!" Shawn said after her first bite.

"And I love the sauce. It's sweet and tangy and the seasonings are just right!" Natasha added.

"I wonder if this place has a cookbook," Molly mused. "Maybe they'll give us some recipes for our Dish cookbook!"

Half an hour later, Vicky returned to their table, this time carrying a large bowl of vanilla ice cream and a deep-dish apple pie. "It's still warm," Vicky told the girls with a smile. "We just took it out of the oven thirty minutes ago!"

"*Mmm*. This is *delicious*," Amanda sighed. The rest of the girls agreed!

After dinner, Omar came up to the Chef Girls' table. "Cheng!" he yelled out. "I challenge you to a game of foosball. Meet me in the rec room in five minutes—*if you dare*."

"Oh, I'll be there," Peichi shot back. "And don't call me Cheng!"

Two hours and several foosball games later, Mr. Degregorio flicked the lights in the rec room on and off. "Okay, everyone," he announced. "Lights out is at ten o'clock. It's time to get bundled up and head back to the cabins."

Several kids groaned, but Amanda leaned over to her

friends and whispered, "Now the *really* fun part starts—our four-day sleepover party!"

Outside, a nearly full moon shone brightly in the night sky. "Wow!" Peichi exclaimed. "It's so *bright* out here from the moon! And there are no streetlights or car lights or anything!"

"Yeah, but it's awfully dark over there," Amanda said, shivering as she pointed toward the forest.

"It's cold, too," Natasha added. "Let's run back to the cabin!"

A few minutes later, the girls arrived at their cabin, breathless from running in the cold air.

"All right! Let the sleepover begin!" Amanda cried, jumping onto her bed.

"Let's get out all of our snacks," Natasha suggested. "Then we can share during the weekend." Soon, there was a huge pile of snacks—chips, soda, cookies, juice boxes, apples, and oranges—on the table.

Mrs. Lopez came in then. "My goodness, that's quite a spread," she said when she saw the pile of food. She glanced at her watch. "Lights out in thirty minutes, girls. I don't mind if you talk quietly before bed. *Quietly.* Good night!"

"Good night, Mrs. Lopez," chorused everyone.

"Thirty minutes? That doesn't give us much time for a sleepover," complained Tessa.

"Not to worry," Amanda replied. She rummaged in one

of her suitcases and pulled out four flashlights and several packages of batteries. "After lights out, we can still have a low-light sleepover! But first things first. Let's change into our pj's and get beautiful while there's still enough light to look in the mirror!"

After the girls had changed into cozy sweats and flannel pajamas, they crowded around the small mirror on the wall.

"You need to take extra-good care of your skin during cold weather," Amanda said importantly. "I read it in one of Mom's magazines. Really cold air makes your skin all dry and icky. That's why I brought all of this stuff!" Amanda dumped her toiletries case onto the bed. Out spilled several small tubes of moisturizer, lotion, and face masks.

"Dry skin is not exactly my problem," Iris laughed. "More like super-oily pimply skin!"

"Yeah, I've been breaking out lately, too," Peichi complained. "What's up with that? My skin was really smooth before and now it's totally gross!"

"Don't worry, I came prepared," Amanda joked. "This cream gets rid of zits practically overnight. It works great!"

"Yeah, right. You don't even have any zits!"

"*Exactly,*" chuckled Amanda as she tossed the tube of cream to Peichi.

Amanda played dermatologist as she examined each one of her friends' faces and prescribed a beauty mask for them. Soon, all the girls were giggling as they applied thick layers of goopy mud, seaweed, or honey masks. Even Molly let Amanda convince her to try a mud mask!

"*Eeek!* This stuff is so slimy!" Peichi squealed as she smeared a drippy seaweed mask onto her face.

"*Shhh!* Don't wake up Mrs. Lopez!" Shawn shushed her.

Suddenly, there was a knock at the door. The girls froze.

"Who-who do you think that is?" Elizabeth asked.

Molly shrugged. "I don't know," she replied. She walked over to the door.

"Molls, don't answer it!" Amanda whispered fiercely. "What if it's, like, an escaped convict or something?"

Molly rolled her eyes. "Oh, *puh-lease,*" she sighed.

There was another knock, and the girls squealed.

"Hey, be cool. It's just me, Connor," came a voice from the other side of the door. The girls giggled with relief.

"I found Natasha's mom's wallet on the path," he said. "But I'm not sure which cabin she's staying in."

"Oh, okay," Molly called out.

She swung open the door just as Amanda squealed, "Molls, no! We're not even—"

Connor, Omar, and Justin jumped into the room.

"Say cheese!" Omar said in a loud whisper. A flash brightened the room, then the boys raced out the door.

"*Ohmigosh!* They just took a picture of us! Looking like *this*!" Amanda shrieked.

"They really, really stink!" Iris exclaimed—but she couldn't stop laughing.

The girls heard Mrs. Lopez's door open. "Girls, what's going on down there?" she called from the top of the steps.

Amanda opened her mouth to reply, but Peichi beat her to it. "Oh, nothing," she called out. "Sorry we were loud. We're just going to finish getting ready for bed and go to sleep. Good night!"

"Good night," Mrs. Lopez called back.

"Peichi! Why didn't you tell her what those jerks did?" Amanda whispered. "They would have gotten seriously busted!"

"I have a better idea," Peichi replied slyly. "We're going to get back at them by getting even—not by telling. Trust me, it will be way more fun!" She switched on her flashlight and turned off the overhead light. "Now, let's come up with some really wicked, really awesome pranks. We'll teach *them* to mess with the girls in Cabin Four!"

T he next morning at breakfast, the Chef Girls were unusually quiet—and extra-tired from staying up late planning pranks. Peichi looked like she was about to fall asleep at the table.

"Look, they just put up today's Chore Chart," Amanda said through a yawn. "I'm going to see what we're doing this morning." She walked across the room to a group of giggling kids in front of the Chore Chart.

"The hardest chore of all is going to be staying awake," Iris sighed. "Why *did* we stay up so late?"

"Don't worry, it will all be worth it," Peichi said sleepily. "I can't wait for Operation Punk the Boys!"

"You look like you can't wait to go to sleep," teased Shawn.

Amanda returned and slapped a Polaroid photo on the table. "Those jerks!" she hissed. "They stuck this picture of us up on the Chore Chart! Everyone was laughing at us!"

The girls leaned in to look at the picture. "*Ohmigosh!*" shrieked Tessa. "Look at all that goop on my face!"

"And my hair is sticking out funny," moaned Natasha.

" 'Someone really needs their beauty sleep,' " Peichi read the photo's caption aloud. "Oh, real funny. I can't wait to get even with those guys!"

"We will—and look on the bright side," Molly pointed out. "Amanda took the picture down before anyone else could see it. Hey, what's our chore for today?"

Amanda wrinkled up her nose. "Ugh—we're doing farming right after breakfast," she complained. "We have to report to the barn. I hope it doesn't stink in there!"

"At least we'll get the farming out of the way," Natasha said practically. "And maybe it won't be so bad."

"Yeah, my grandparents used to have a farm in Minnesota," Elizabeth spoke up. "I would help them out during the summers. It was pretty cool!"

After the girls had finished their breakfasts, they bundled up in their heavy winter gear. On the way to the barn, they ran into Angie and her crew.

"Hey, Shawn! Saw you're farming today. Have fun in the barn! I bet there are some pigs you could play with. You don't seem very picky about who you're friends with!" Angie yelled.

Shawn turned her head so she couldn't see Angie. *Don't get into it. Keep your mouth shut*, she thought over and over.

But Amanda couldn't resist. "Saw you're cleaning today. Have fun with that, Angie. You'll fit right in with the dirt and the muck."

"You better watch your mouth," Angie shot back.

"This is insane," Molly whispered. "Let's just get out of here."

The girls walked silently toward the barn. Finally, Shawn spoke. "Amanda, I really appreciate you sticking up for me with Angie. But listen, it's not worth it. She'll just go after you."

"Yeah, and she's completely evil," Elizabeth said quietly.

"I know how Angie is," Amanda replied. "But I get so mad when she treats you like that, Shawn. I can't help saying something back to her."

"I know," Shawn said simply. "But I don't mind ignoring her. If nobody responds, then she'll get bored and start picking on someone else."

"Anyway, let's forget about her for now," Molly said. "Hopefully, we won't see her again for the rest of the day."

At the barn, Mr. Hudson was waiting for the girls, along with two helpers. "Welcome, ladies!" Mr. Hudson called out. "The other group is already here. This is the animal's cabin, as we like to call it," he chuckled. "Come on inside."

Inside the barn, it took a few moments for the girls' eyes to adjust to the dim light. It was warm and quiet, except for the soft animal noises, and it smelled like hay and manure.

"Wow! It's much bigger in here than it looks from the outside!" Peichi exclaimed.

Mr. Hudson chuckled. "We keep a lot of animals in here—six cows, four horses, and eight sheep. There's a whole flock of chickens in the loft, too."

"Cool!" said one of the boys from the other group.

"Back in colonial days, settlers relied on their animals for food, warmth, help with farming, transportation, and even clothing. Our animals are the same breeds many settlers had then—Red Devon cows, Leicester Longwool sheep, and Dorking chickens."

"Dorking chickens?" called one of the guys, laughing.

Mr. Hudson grinned. "I agree—an unfortunate name. Well, let's begin! This is a pretty large group, so everyone can take turns doing the winter barnyard activities. Let's number off in threes."

After everyone had called out a one, two, or three, Mr. Hudson said, "Okay, ones follow Thomas upstairs to collect eggs from the chicken roost. Twos, start shoveling out the stalls and adding fresh hay—Lois will show you where the pitchforks are. And, threes, come with me—we'll start you off on milking the cows. We'll switch roles in about thirty minutes."

"Oh, man," Amanda whispered to Molly. "I should have known I'd get stuck with the cows!"

"We'll all have to try the milking eventually," Molly whispered back. "Go, Manda! You'll be great!"

Milking the cows wasn't nearly as gross as Amanda thought it would be. First, Mr. Hudson had her give the cow a bale of fresh hay to munch on. "That keeps her calm," he explained. Next, Amanda had to wash the cow's udder with warm water. Then, Mr. Hudson showed her how to milk the cow using gentle pressure. Before she knew it, her tin pail was filled with fresh, creamy milk.

Searching for eggs in the chicken roost was actually fun. "It's like an Easter egg hunt," Elizabeth said to Molly. But cleaning out the stalls and filling them with fresh hay was hard work—and smelly, too.

"I had no idea straw could be so heavy," Peichi grunted as she struggled to lift a pitchfork with a pile of clean straw on it. "This is hard work!"

"It *is* hard," Mr. Hudson said. "Colonial farmers started their days well before dawn, and often didn't get to bed until after dark. There was almost always more work than people to do it.

"All righty, everybody," Mr. Hudson called to the rest of the group. "It's twelve-thirty now, so why don't you all run along and get cleaned up for lunch? You've all worked real hard. Have a great time on the slopes!"

After lunch, the Chef Girls couldn't wait to hit the slopes. They hurried back to their cabin to change into their ski gear.

As they stepped outside, Natasha suddenly turned pale. "*Ohmigosh!*" she whispered. "Look at my parents!"

Mr. and Mrs. Ross were approaching Cabin Four, wearing shiny, brand-new ski suits in shocking shades of lime green and bright yellow. Mrs. Ross waved her ski pole in the air and called out, "Yoo-hoo! Natasha! Are you ready to check out the powder on those cool slopes?"

Some students passing by the Rosses started to snicker, but Natasha's parents didn't seem to notice.

Natasha winced. "Oh, man, this is so embarrassing," she moaned.

"I think it's really sweet that your parents wanted to come on the trip with you," Elizabeth said.

"Me, too," Molly said. She glanced at Amanda. "Well, we're gonna take off for the intermediate slopes. Who wants to come?"

"I will!" said Peichi and Shawn.

"I'm gonna be stuck on the bunny slopes with my parents," sighed Natasha.

"Don't worry," Elizabeth said. "I'll stick with you."

"So will I," announced Iris and Tessa.

"Whoopsie!"

Natasha looked over to see her mother flat on her back in a snowdrift, her arms and legs flailing as Mr. Ross tried to help her out. Mrs. Ross, normally so poised and graceful, was a complete klutz on skis!

Here we go, thought Natasha as she tried not to roll her eyes. *It's going to be a long afternoon.*

Shawn, Peichi, and the twins had a blast on the

intermediate slopes. It took them a few tries to remember how to walk in skis by sliding each foot forward instead of lifting it—each girl stumbled a bit at first—but before long they were zooming down the mountain.

"This is so great!" Molly yelled as she skied down the slope, making small turns by leaning on one leg, then the other. "I feel like I'm flying!"

"Why haven't we gone skiing in such a long time?" Amanda asked as she came to a stop at the bottom of the slope by snowplowing—keeping the front of her skis together while sliding the backs of the skis apart to form a V-shape. "We're gonna have to remind Mom and Dad how much fun this is."

The twins waited at the bottom of the mountain until Peichi and Shawn had skied down it, then all the girls took the ski lift back up the mountain together. Molly glanced over at the Five Point slope, which the kids were forbidden to ski down. "It doesn't look so bad over there," she mused. "I wonder why it's off-limits."

"Molls, are you nuts?" Amanda asked. "People can *die* on really hard slopes."

Molly shrugged. "I wouldn't be scared to try it."

"I'm not *scared*," Amanda snapped. "I just think that the intermediate slope is enough."

"Okay, okay," Peichi interrupted. "It doesn't matter, since we can't try it anyway. Right?"

"Right," the twins agreed at the same time.

Peichi checked her digital watch. "Hey, it's already four o'clock," she said. "Come on, Amanda, we have to get back for Operation Punk the Boys."

Amanda giggled. "Right! I almost forgot!" She turned to Molly and Shawn. "We have to perform our important mission. See you guys back at the cabin. Come on, Peichi, one more run!" She and Peichi took off down the slope.

Molly and Shawn giggled as they remembered the prank Amanda had come up with the night before. "This is gonna be good!" Molly said.

Shawn grinned. "I know. I can't wait for dinner!"

At the bottom of the slope, Amanda and Peichi told one of the ski instructors that they were cold and tired and wanted to rest before dinner. Then they walked casually to their cabin, trying not to laugh too much on the way.

"Keep an eye out for the chaperones," Amanda said to Peichi as they entered their cabin. Peichi stood near the front window, watching the trail, as Amanda hurried over to her makeup case. "Found it!" Amanda cried triumphantly, holding up a small tube of nail glue.

"The coast is clear," Peichi said. "To the lodge!"

The girls walked quickly down the path. Peichi continued to look out for any grown-ups, but the lodge was empty and quiet. The tables had already been set for dinner.

"Fifth table from the front," Amanda muttered to herself as she unscrewed the cap of the nail glue. She found the seats where Omar, Connor, and Justin had sat for the past three meals, and quickly glued their napkins, silverware, and plates to the place mats. She looked over her shoulder at Peichi, who gave her the thumbs-up sign. *Why quit now?* Amanda thought mischievously, loosening the tops of the salt and pepper shakers.

Amanda stood back to admire her work. *This is gonna be hysterical!* she thought. Then, a strange noise that sounded like an owl caught her attention. She turned around to see Peichi hooting at her.

Amanda frowned and hurried over to Peichi. "What are you doing?" she whispered. *"Shhh!"*

"That's the code," Peichi explained. "Hooting like an owl means, 'Time to go!' Mission accomplished?"

"Absolutely!" Amanda replied.

"Then let's get out of here!"

Amanda and Peichi raced back to their cabin, not daring to laugh along the way. Finally, they reached Cabin Four and burst through the doors to find the rest of their bunkmates eagerly waiting for them.

"Well? Did you do it? Did you do it?" Molly asked excitedly.

Amanda nodded, laughing too hard to speak. The girls in the cabin started screaming and jumping up and down.

"Oh, I can't wait to see their faces when they realize their forks are glued to the table!" Elizabeth squealed.

"Serves them right for taking that terrible picture of us and showing the whole school," Tessa added.

Amanda took a deep breath and tried to calm down. "Now all we have to do is hope they sit at the same table."

"Oh, they will," Natasha spoke up. "Those guys sit at the exact same table in the cafeteria every day."

The other girls looked at her, and Natasha blushed.

"It's just something I noticed, is all," she stammered.

When the friends got to the dining room for dinner, they could barely contain their anticipation. "Remember, act normal. Don't laugh," Amanda advised everyone as she tried to hold back a grin.

But for Peichi, it was too much. As Omar, Justin, and Connor entered the room, she had to bite her lip to stop herself from giggling.

"Keep it together, Peichi," Molly whispered. "Look! They're going over there!"

The three boys sat at their table—right in the spots where Amanda had glued the tableware!

"They don't have a clue!" Shawn whispered gleefully.

"Oh, this is gonna be so great," Amanda whispered back. Then she cleared her throat and tried to speak in a normal voice. "So, did everybody learn a lot today?" But that only made her friends start laughing.

The waiters and waitresses started bringing in large tureens of steaming soup, baskets of crusty bread, and large bowls of salad. The girls saw Omar say, "Awesome!" as a waiter approached his table.

Then he tried to pick up his spoon. Omar's face twisted in confusion as he tried to pry his spoon off the place mat. Then Connor and Justin tried to pick up their spoons, too— then their forks, glasses, and napkins.

Peichi's face turned bright red and she started laughing—until Molly kicked her lightly under the table.

Just then, Omar looked up and caught Peichi's eye. She could tell from his face that he knew she was involved. He nodded his head once and pointed at her.

"You guys! Omar just pointed at me! He knows!" Peichi whispered.

"Just act normal," Natasha advised, staring down at her plate. She didn't know *what* would happen if she looked at Connor!

Across the room, Omar spoke quietly to his waiter, who tried not to laugh as he discreetly cleared the glued place settings off the table.

"Whoa. Could we get in trouble for gluing the stuff down?" Natasha asked, suddenly serious. "It belongs to Mr. and Mrs. Hudson."

Amanda's eyes grew wide. "I didn't think of that. Now I feel really bad!"

"Maybe we can apologize and pay for the silverware," Molly said, thinking aloud.

"But what if we get in trouble and they send us home?" Peichi asked. "They're really strict with the rules on school trips."

"We can probably get the silverware off the place mats," Amanda pointed out. "We just have to soak everything in hot water for a while—that makes the glue dissolve. Molls...would you go ask that waiter for the place mats? Pretty please?"

Molly rolled her eyes. "*You* glued the stuff down. You do it."

Amanda sighed dramatically, then flounced across the room to the waiter. Her friends watched as the waiter, still grinning, handed Amanda the rolled-up place mats and silverware. Amanda quickly smuggled them back to her table.

"Nice job, Amanda!" cheered Natasha.

"It was a piece of cake. I think that waiter thought it was really funny."

"Still, we should fix it," Shawn pointed out.

"And be more careful with our other pranks," Natasha added.

After dinner, the friends hurried back to their cabin to soak the place mats and silverware in the sink, then played Monopoly for several hours in the lodge until, once again, Mr. D. flicked the lights on and off to

announce lights out. They'd had such a great time that they didn't notice Omar sneak out of the lodge for several minutes.

"Hey—did somebody leave the light on?" Molly asked as the girls walked toward their cabin.

"I don't think so," Iris replied.

"That's really weird," Natasha said with a frown. "I'm sure we turned off the lights."

The girls cautiously entered their cabin. "Well, there's no one here," Molly announced after looking around. "We must have left the light on."

"Hey, Peichi—what's that?" Shawn asked, pointing at a folded piece of notebook paper on Peichi's bed.

"Looks like a note or something," Peichi replied as she unfolded the paper.

"A *love* note?" Amanda asked, grinning.

"Yeah, right," Peichi snorted. Suddenly, her face twisted into a frown. "*Ohmigosh!* I am *so* gonna get Omar!" she shrieked.

"What happened?" chorused her bunkmates.

"He kidnapped Moosie!" Peichi replied as she started

frantically rummaging through her suitcase. "*Oooh*, he is gonna get it!"

"Who's Moosie?" asked the twins at the same time, trying not to laugh.

Peichi looked up, embarrassed. "He's—he's my favorite stuffed animal since I was a baby," she replied. "I, uh, I still sleep with him sometimes. That's pretty lame, I guess."

The twins exchanged a smile. "No, we still have all our old stuffed animals," Amanda quickly said.

"Yeah, but you don't sleep with them! What if Omar tells everybody I brought this old stuffed moose on the trip? Everyone will laugh at me! And what's he gonna do to poor Moosie? I can't *believe* he kidnapped my Moosie!"

"Chill, Peichi," Shawn said sweetly. "We'll get your Moosie back. And we'll get even!"

chapter 8

Omar seemed to have his own plans for Moosie. The next morning, Peichi found a Polaroid picture next to her plate. It was of Moosie—standing on a snowboard! Peichi couldn't help laughing as she passed the picture around to her friends.

"The guys must have gotten up pretty early to take this picture," Amanda said. She was just joining the table after returning the un-stuck silverware and place mats from their prank.

"Getting up early...hey, that gives me an idea!" Peichi said excitedly. "I know how we can get back at them. Here's the plan: we—"

"Hi, Mom!" Natasha yelled so loudly that kids at nearby tables turned to look at her.

Wide-eyed, Peichi turned around to see Mrs. Ross standing behind her. *Yipes!* Peichi thought. *Did she hear me? I hope not!*

Mrs. Ross smiled and greeted the girls good morning. Then, she sat down at the table with them!

Poor Natasha, Peichi thought. *You can tell she's embarrassed. Kind of like the way I feel about Moosie being on the loose...I'll have to tell her that later!*

Fortunately, Mrs. Ross didn't stay long. "I saw on the Chore Chart that you girls have cooking today," she said brightly. "I'm sure tonight's meal will be the most delicious one yet! Now, tell me, are you all having a good time? Are you warm enough? Do you need anything at all?"

"We're fine, thanks," Amanda spoke up, remembering her manners. "Are you having a good time?"

Mrs. Ross nodded. "Oh, yes, it's beautiful up here," she said. "Though I must admit, I prefer golf to skiing. Well, if any of you need *anything*, don't hesitate to ask Mr. Ross or me. We promised your parents we'd take good care of you." She leaned over to kiss Natasha on the cheek, then said, "Bye-bye! Have fun in the kitchen!"

As soon as her mother was out of sight, Natasha buried her head in her hands. "*Argh!*" she moaned. "I'm sorry, guys. It's bad enough my mom treats *me* like a baby. But she should leave you guys alone!"

"No, Natasha, it's fine," Molly said. "We don't mind."

"Yeah," echoed Elizabeth. "It's kind of nice, the way your mom wants to look after you."

Natasha remembered how Elizabeth had lost both of her parents in a car accident when she was just a baby, and immediately felt guilty. *Real nice,* she chided herself. *You keep complaining about your parents, and Elizabeth doesn't even have hers.* Natasha decided then that she would stop complaining about her mom and dad—no matter how embarrassing they were.

The girls spent the morning on the slopes again. After lunch, they walked through the back of the dining room to the kitchen.

"I wonder what we'll have to do to cook 'colonially,'" Molly said. "Like, will we churn our own butter?"

"Well, we milked our own cows yesterday," Amanda joked. "So I wouldn't be surprised if we have to churn our own butter, too!"

"Actually, all the milk our cows make is processed at Green Mountain Dairy down the road." Mrs. Hudson entered the kitchen, tying an apron around her neck. "So we don't have to churn our own butter, thankfully—it's an awfully hard job! Now, let's see, would everyone please write their names down on a name tag? We'll begin as soon as the other group gets here."

As Molly wondered which group would join them, the doors burst open. Angie strode into the kitchen, followed by the other cheerleaders in her cabin.

Shawn winced. The Chef Girls exchanged glances that said, *Oh, no!*

"Excellent! Everyone's here!" Mrs. Hudson exclaimed. "I always begin the cooking sessions by giving a tour of what a colonial kitchen was like. Women did virtually all of the cooking. Ovens and stoves were rare—women usually cooked right over an open fire. It was a dangerous life. Many women died when their long dresses caught fire.

"Almost all kitchen utensils were made of wood—pewter tools were very expensive. Because cooking can be dangerous, we'll be using modern tools. But our recipes are authentic! We'll make corn chowder, fried chicken with cornmeal coating, mashed potatoes, and spiced carrot cake."

After the tour, Mrs. Hudson assigned the kids to different jobs. Shawn was relieved to not be in Angie's group. *Hopefully, we can just stay out of each other's way and everything will be fine,* Shawn thought as she started grating carrots for the cake.

And everything *was* fine—until Shawn noticed Angie putting the cooked chicken back in the pan that had held the raw chicken pieces. "Angie! Don't do that!" Shawn called across the kitchen.

Everyone stopped what they were doing and turned to stare at Shawn, then Angie. Angie's eyes narrowed. She looked angrier than Shawn had ever seen her.

"What's the problem, Shawn?" Angie snapped, her face turning red.

"Um, you're not supposed to put cooked meat back in the same dish that held raw meat," Shawn tried to explain gently. "If the raw meat had any germs in it, the germs get all over the cooked meat. That's one way people can get food poisoning."

"Oh, yeah. *Thanks*, Shawn. You're such a *big* help," Angie sneered. "If you think you could do such a *great* job, why don't you just do it yourself?" She threw her apron on the ground and stormed out of the kitchen, her long hair flying behind her.

Everyone was silent for a moment.

"Well, goodness," said Mrs. Hudson. "Shawn, would you please take over the fried chicken for us?"

Shawn nodded silently. As she passed Mrs. Hudson, she whispered, "I'm sorry. I was only trying to help."

"No apologies necessary, dear! I'm glad you noticed. It would have been *terrible* if people had gotten sick." Mrs. Hudson smiled at Shawn, but it only made her feel a little better.

That night at dinner, Peichi found another picture of Moosie at her place. This time, he was ice fishing with a tiny pole made out of a twig, with a paper fish taped to the end of the line. The girls cracked up as they passed the photo around.

"Omar's going all out for this one," Molly said. "I have to admit, I'm impressed."

"I'm impressed with the dinner we made!" Elizabeth exclaimed. "I've never cooked anything like this before. It's so good!"

"Looks like everyone agrees with you," Amanda said as she watched the other students and the chaperones eagerly eating the corn chowder and fried chicken.

"Everyone except Angie," Shawn said in a quiet voice. "She's only eating the salad."

Amanda rolled her eyes. "Seriously, she is such a baby," she whispered across the table. "I couldn't believe the way she acted earlier. Like, grow up! It would have been so much worse if Shawn *didn't* tell her about it. What if everybody got sick?"

"I guess Angie doesn't think like that," Elizabeth spoke up. "She was only thinking about herself."

"Listen, not to totally change the subject or anything," Peichi interrupted, "but who cares about Angie? We have *bigger* things to talk about. Like our prank tonight! *Ooooh*, it's gonna be so funny!"

"Okay, okay," Molly said with a laugh. "What's the plan?"

"This one is called...Attack of the Alarm Clocks," Peichi whispered, her eyes twinkling. "We only need one alarm clock in our cabin, right? But we all brought one."

"Well, Amanda and I are sharing one," Molly said.

Peichi waved her hand. "Doesn't matter. We still have six extra travel alarm clocks. So, after dinner, we'll sneak into the guys' cabin and hide the alarm clocks all over the place. And each one will be set for a different time. So they'll be ringing at crazy hours all night long—

midnight, one a.m., two-thirty a.m., three a.m.! And besides being woken up, like, six times during the middle of the night, they'll have to find the alarm clocks before they can even turn them off! It's gonna be *great!*" Peichi paused to take a deep breath, and the girls laughed.

"I love it! It's genius!" Amanda cried.

"So, here's what I was thinking," Peichi continued. "We should have two people hide the clocks. And two people can be lookouts. How does that sound?"

"I'll be a lookout," Natasha quickly volunteered.

"Me, too," Elizabeth said.

"Okay, I want to hide the clocks," Peichi said.

"So do I!" Molly exclaimed.

"Sweet! Okay, at seven-thirty, the four of us should start to casually leave the lodge. Just one at a time, so no one gets suspicious. Then we'll meet back at our cabin to set the alarms and get our flashlights."

"Peichi, I'm impressed," Iris said with a smile. "You've really thought this through."

"You bet!" Peichi said cheerfully. "I just wish we could be there to see the guys' faces every time the alarms go off!"

A few hours later, Molly, Peichi, Natasha, and Elizabeth huddled outside the boys' cabin, ready to sneak inside.

"Natasha and Elizabeth, stand on either side of the path," whispered Peichi. "Pretend like you're walking to the lodge if anyone comes by. If there's trouble, start talking really loud. Or hoot like an owl. Like this—*hoot! Hoot!*"

The girls tried to muffle their laughter, and Peichi rolled her eyes. "Okay, okay," she said. "Just make sure you let us know if anyone is coming. We could get seriously busted if anyone finds us in the boys' cabin."

"Got it," Natasha replied, nodding seriously.

"All right! Let's do this!" Peichi whispered.

Silently, Molly and Peichi snuck into the boys' cabin and turned on their flashlights. They scurried around the room, searching for the most difficult hiding places they could find. Peichi hid her first clock in the far corner of the room, behind someone's suitcase; Molly hid one under a bed and another in a drawer of clothes, making sure to leave the drawer open just a bit so the sound would come through.

Peichi wanted to hide her last clock in the perfect place. She spotted a rectangular black case near someone's bed. *Great!* she thought. *I'll hide the alarm clock in here, then hide the case!* She quickly unzipped it, then covered up her mouth to keep from laughing.

"Check it out!" she whispered. "This case is full of shaving stuff! As if!"

Molly giggled. "I wonder which one of the guys pretends that he needs to shave," she said slyly.

Suddenly, Natasha's voice rang through the cabin. "Oh, hi, Connor!"

The girls froze.

Yipes! What are we gonna do now? Molly wondered, staring at Peichi with wide eyes.

"Sure! I'd love to go for a walk!" Natasha yelled.

Peichi crept over to the window.

"Natasha's leaving with Connor," she reported in a whisper. "We'd better get out of here! Are all the clocks hidden? Okay, let's go!"

Molly and Peichi snuck out of the cabin and raced down the path with Elizabeth. When they reached the safety of their own cabin, they slammed the door behind them and started laughing hysterically.

"What happened? What happened?" Amanda shrieked.

"*Ohmigosh*, we almost got caught!" Peichi squealed. "Connor came down the path! But Natasha intercepted him, and they went on a walk or something."

"They went on a walk?" Shawn asked. "That's weird."

Elizabeth pressed her hand over her chest. "Can you believe we almost got caught? Imagine if Connor had been with the rest of the guys! Or if their chaperone had come back!"

"That was a really close call," Molly agreed. "But what a blast!"

"I wonder where Natasha and Connor are going," Peichi said.

"We'll just have to ask her all about it when she gets back," Amanda said.

Connor didn't say much as he and Natasha walked along the path. "So, um, where are we going?" she finally asked.

"It's just up here a little way," replied Connor. They passed Natasha's cabin and came to a fork in the path. Natasha had never been down this way before.

Suddenly, Connor grabbed her arm. "Right here," he said, gesturing out to a small clearing between the mountains. The full moon shone brightly on the untouched snow, which glittered like a million tiny diamonds.

"Wow," Natasha breathed. "It's so beautiful!"

"Yeah," Connor said softly. "I took a walk out here last night. When I saw it, I thought of you. I, um, I thought you might like to see it."

Natasha's cheeks had turned pink from the cold, and her pale blue eyes sparkled. "Thanks for showing me. It's amazing."

They stood for a minute in silence. Eventually, Natasha turned to Connor to suggest they go back to camp, when, to her surprise, he leaned over and quickly brushed his lips against hers.

Whoa, Natasha thought, stunned. *I didn't see that coming! What do I do now?*

"Are you, um, mad?" Connor asked nervously.

"No, I'm just, uh, surprised," Natasha replied, blinking.

"Natasha?" asked a voice behind them.

Natasha turned around to see someone standing behind them on the path.

It was Mrs. Ross!

Oh, no! She must have seen Connor kiss me!

"Would you come here, please?" Mrs. Ross asked formally, a forced smile on her face.

Connor's eyes grew wide. "Uh, see you tomorrow, Natasha. Good night, Mrs. Ross," he stammered before hurrying away.

"Come back to my cabin. I want to talk to you," Mrs. Ross said firmly.

Uh-oh, she's really mad, Natasha thought as she climbed the stairs to Mrs. Ross's loft.

"Exactly what is going on? Who was that? Was that that Connor boy? How long has this been going on? Natasha, I am just *shocked* that you have been sneaking around like this! When I tell your father—"

"Wait, wait, wait, wait!" Natasha interrupted her mother. "Stop jumping to all these conclusions! Connor just told me he wanted to show me something, and then he suddenly leaned over and kissed me. I'm as surprised as you are!" Natasha looked her mother straight in the eye. "Please don't be so *suspicious* of me! I don't sneak around on you and Dad. But—I need some privacy!"

"*Privacy*? Natasha, I'm your mother. It's my job to keep you out of trouble!"

"But why do you think I'm going to get into trouble?" Natasha asked. "I've always been a good kid. You can't stop trusting me just because I'm a teenager now!"

Mrs. Ross sighed deeply and rubbed her temples. "Honestly, Natasha, I just don't know if I'm ready to deal with you and *boys*," she said.

"I know, Mom," Natasha said quietly. "Molly and Amanda's mom doesn't let them date." She took a deep breath. "I...like Connor. I do. And I guess he likes me, too. But there's nothing else going on. I promise. And if he *does* ask me out or anything, I'll tell you all about it."

Mrs. Ross smiled at Natasha. "You'll always be my little girl, sweetheart. That's why it's easy for me to forget you're growing up. You'll have to help me through it, okay? Let's make a deal—you'll keep Daddy and me informed, and we won't jump to conclusions. And we'll try to respect your privacy. Okay?"

"Okay, Mom," Natasha replied, smiling. "I love you."

"I love you, Natasha," Mrs. Ross replied, brushing Natasha's bangs off her forehead. "Well, it's almost nine o'clock. I'll walk you back to your cabin."

"Just partway?"

"Okay." Mrs. Ross chuckled. "I can do that."

Late that night, after the other girls in Cabin Four had fallen asleep, Natasha lay awake, thinking about Connor—and about her first kiss. Natasha hadn't told anyone else about it. It seemed too private, too special to share with the entire bunk.

I can't believe he kissed me! Natasha thought dreamily. *I wonder if he uses ChapStick. He smelled nice, too. Like apple soap or something...*

Though Natasha had promised her mother that she wouldn't start dating, she couldn't help but wish she could kiss Connor again. *Maybe someday*, she thought, a small smile creeping over her face.

chapter 9

"**L**ook! Here they come!" Peichi said excitedly the next morning. Breakfast was almost over and Omar, Connor, Justin, and the rest of their cabin were straggling in the door.

"*Awww*, they look exhausted!" Amanda said, giggling. "I almost feel bad. Almost!"

Natasha saw Connor looking at her. She mouthed the word, "Sorry!" to him as he grinned at her. *Oh, good, he's not mad,* Natasha thought, relieved. She looked down shyly, remembering their moment in the moonlight.

"Look at Omar's face!" Peichi said. "He'll do something crazy to get back at us. We'd better be on our guard."

"And let's think up another prank," added Molly. "I can't believe we're leaving tomorrow! This weekend has flown by."

"And it's been so much fun, too," Natasha said.

"Well, this morning isn't gonna be fun," Amanda said, making a face. "We've got cleaning duty—ugh! I can't imagine cleaning without our vacuum and ScumBuster."

After lunch, the girls went back to their cabin to change into their ski gear. When Molly opened the door, her mouth fell open.

"How did they do it?" she asked, amazed.

"Do what?" Amanda pushed past her sister and stopped in the middle of the room. *"Ohmigosh!"* she shrieked. "Those guys are totally out of control!"

The rest of the girls hurried into the cabin, and burst out laughing when they saw an enormous, five-foot snowman in the center of the room. It had a face made out of rocks and sticks, and was wearing a Yankees baseball cap.

Shawn shivered. "They must have turned off the heat—it's freezing in here! That's why it hasn't melted."

"That's Omar's hat," Peichi exclaimed, grabbing the Yankees cap off the snowman's head.

"Look at how they put these trash bags on the floor under it," Natasha marveled. "They really thought of everything!"

"Well, we've got to get it out of here," Iris said practically.

"I have an idea!" Molly exclaimed. "Let's take off the head and middle. Then we can roll the base out. We'll reassemble the snowman right outside our door."

"Might as well," Peichi said. "They worked so hard on this prank—now we're gonna have to think of something really good!"

Fifteen minutes later, the girls had reassembled the snowman outside. Omar, Justin, and Connor walked by casually, pretending that they were on their way to the slopes. "Hey—cool snowdude!" Omar called to the girls. "How'd you make it so big?"

"Ha ha, Omar," Peichi retorted. "Are you missing something?" She waved his Yankees cap high in the air.

"Peichi! You found my hat! Oh, thank you so much!" Omar tried to grab his hat, but Peichi held it out of his reach and jumped back.

"I don't think so, Omar," she said.

"Aw, come on, Cheng," Omar grinned. "Don't make me come get it." He reached down and scooped up a big handful of snow.

"Okay, okay," Peichi said, thrusting the hat at Omar.

Omar grabbed his hat, bent the brim a few times, and put it on over his ski cap. "Thanks, Peichi. You're my hero! Truce?"

"Yeah, right," Peichi replied with a mischievous smile.

Omar looked so goofy wearing the two hats that everyone cracked up.

"Listen, we're gonna hit the slopes one more time," Justin spoke up. "It looks like it's going to snow this afternoon, so we'd better get out there. Want to come?"

"Sure," Natasha said quickly. She caught Connor's eye and smiled at him.

"Actually, I think I'm going to hang out in the lodge

this afternoon," Shawn said. "It's too cold for me." She grabbed a book from her backpack.

"Okay, Shawn, we'll see you at dinner—maybe before, if it starts snowing," said Amanda. The girls and the boys trudged toward the slope, while Shawn set off for the lodge.

On the way, Shawn saw Angie and her crew walking toward the slopes, as well. *Uh-oh*, Shawn thought, her heart starting to beat a little faster. *Just keep walking, Angie. Please just leave me alone.*

But Angie couldn't resist a chance to taunt Shawn. "Hey, Shawn! What are you doing all by yourself?" she called out loudly.

"I'm just going to hang out in the lodge and read," Shawn answered, hoping her voice sounded normal.

"Oh, okay," Angie replied. "I was afraid that your other friends had dumped you, too." Shrieking with laughter, Angie continued down the path, leaving Shawn to stand alone, red-faced and shaking.

Maybe it will never stop, Shawn thought sadly as she reached the lodge. *Maybe Angie will keep picking on me for the rest of middle school...and then high school...maybe she will never stop.*

Three hours later, the first snowflakes started falling. Shawn, wrapped up in her book, didn't even notice. She was the only person in the rec room, and it felt so relaxing to be by herself for a little while, curled up in a comfy over-stuffed armchair.

Suddenly, the door to the rec room burst open, and Angie ran in.

"Shawn! Shawn!" she shrieked breathlessly.

"What? What is it?" Shawn asked warily, sitting up.

"*Oh*, it's so horrible. Amanda tried to ski down the Five Point slope and she hit a tree! She's crying and bleeding and I think her leg is broken or something. She's asking for you, Shawn. You've got to go sit with her while I get help!"

"*Ohmigosh*," Shawn gasped, dropping her book. She threw on her parka and began tying her bootlaces. "Where is she? Did you call an ambulance?"

"She's on the far side of the slope, near the bottom. You can go through the woods to get to her. Molly is with her, but—but it looks pretty bad." Angie bit her lip and looked genuinely worried. "I have to go get Mr. D."

"Thanks so much for finding me, Angie," Shawn said gratefully as she ran out of the room.

Outside, Shawn ran as fast as she could, her feet weighed down by the heavy snow boots.

By the time Shawn got to the woods, the snow was falling faster. She brushed the powdery flakes out of her eyes and pushed through the low branches of some large pine trees. Shawn's heart pounded faster and faster as she imagined Amanda, in pain, crying. Finally, she saw a speck of light ahead and realized she must be at the Five Point slope.

Shawn sucked in her breath sharply as she looked up the mountain. It looked terrifying—incredibly steep, studded with gnarled trees and rocks half-covered with snow. *Oh, Amanda,* Shawn thought. *Why would you ever try to ski down* this?

"Amanda! Molly!" Shawn yelled. *"Amanda!"*

There was no answer.

There was no sound at all, except for the whistling wind.

Shawn shivered, but only partly from cold. "Amanda?" she called again. "Amanda, where are you?"

Nothing.

It's so quiet up here, Shawn realized. *I should be able to hear them, especially if Amanda is crying. And they should be able to hear me...*

A terrible thought began to dawn on Shawn. *Unless they aren't up here.* Suddenly, it all made sense to Shawn. *There's no way Amanda would ski down this slope. She didn't even want to.*

Shawn picked up a rock and threw it. She'd never felt so angry before in her life. "I hate you, Angie!" she screamed into the wind. She pictured Angie back at the cozy lodge, telling everyone that Shawn was a total idiot, making fun of her to the entire seventh-grade class.

Shawn took a deep breath and tried to calm down. *It's*

freezing here, she thought, shivering again. *And creepy, too. It's like there's no one else in the world, except for me.* Shawn stomped back into the woods, hurrying toward the lodge.

It was nearly dark now, and the snow was falling heavily. The canopy of thick pines blocked out the last of the daylight. Shawn tried to walk in a straight line through the woods, but found herself wandering in circles. Soon, the woods were completely dark.

Shawn slumped against the trunk of a large tree and shivered uncontrollably from cold and from fear. *I'm lost in the woods, in a snowstorm...*

And no one knows where I am.

"I can't believe how cold it got out there!" Amanda exclaimed as she changed her clothes before dinner. "Look—my toes are bright pink, and I was wearing two pairs of socks under my boots!"

"I heard Mr. Hudson say that the storm might turn into a blizzard," Peichi reported. "Wouldn't that be cool? What if we got stuck here an extra day!"

"*Oooh,* I'll keep my fingers crossed!" cried Iris.

"I am *so* hungry!" Natasha said. "Let's hurry over to the lodge. We can hang out with Shawn before dinner."

At the lodge, the girls searched the dining room and the rec room, but there was no sign of Shawn.

"That's weird. Did we pass her on the way from the cabin?" asked Molly.

"I didn't see her," Amanda replied doubtfully.

Elizabeth checked her watch. "Dinner is in half an hour. I'm sure she'll be back."

The twins exchanged a glance. "You know, I think I'll go back to the cabin real quick to see if she's there," Molly said.

"Me, too," Amanda and Natasha quickly said as Peichi nodded her head.

109

Tessa shrugged. "Okay. See you in the dining room!"

The Chef Girls trudged through the snow back to their cabin, only to find it dark and deserted. For a moment, no one spoke.

"Well, maybe she went outside for something, and then went right back to the lodge," Peichi finally said.

"Maybe," Molly and Amanda said together—but it was obvious they weren't convinced.

The girls hurried back through the falling snow. From outside, the lodge glowed with warm light, and they could see several students through the windows, laughing and having a great time.

She's got to be in the lodge—where else would she be? Molly thought.

It was just after six, and the dining room was filled with hungry students eagerly awaiting dinner. The Chef Girls hurried over to their usual table, where Iris, Tessa, and Elizabeth were waiting for them.

Shawn wasn't there.

"This is seriously weird," Molly said with a frown. "Shawn wasn't at the cabin. And she *knows* dinner is at six."

"I'm worried," Amanda said bluntly.

"Okay," Natasha said slowly. "Um, I'm sure there's nothing to worry about. But I'll tell my mom anyway."

Natasha crossed the room to the table where the chaperones and teachers were having dinner. The adults stopped eating and looked at her as she approached.

"Hi, sweetie," Mr. Ross said cheerfully. "How is everything?"

"Um, fine," Natasha replied cautiously, wishing that all the adults weren't staring at her. "But, um, we can't find Shawn."

"What do you mean, sweetheart?" Mrs. Ross asked, raising her eyebrows.

"Well, she didn't come skiing with us this afternoon. She just wanted to read her book in the rec room," Natasha explained. "And after we got back, we couldn't find her. She's not in our cabin and she's not anywhere in the lodge." She stopped to take a breath, realizing how scary her words sounded.

"All right. Let's just stay calm," Mrs. Ross said in an even voice.

But Mr. Hudson, Mr. Degregorio, and Detective McElroy were already on their feet. "We'll need half the chaperones to search the cabins," Mr. Hudson said. "I'll check the barn. Faith, would you check the kitchen and search through the lodge one more time?"

Mrs. Hudson hurried toward the kitchen, and half of the chaperones went to put on their coats. Natasha sat down heavily next to her mother.

Mrs. Ross put her arm around her daughter. "Try not to worry, sweetheart," she said. "I'm sure Shawn is fine."

Molly and Amanda hurried over to the table. "What's going on?" Molly asked in a low voice.

"They're searching all the buildings on the grounds," Mrs. Ross replied as she stroked Natasha's hair. "Perhaps she fell asleep and missed dinner."

Fifteen minutes later, all of the adults were back in the dining room. Detective McElroy came up to the chaperones' table.

"She's not in any of the buildings," he said in a low voice. "Mr. D., I need you to call her parents. Explain that we're not sure where she is, but we're organizing a search party. Tell them to stay in Brooklyn for now; we'll call with an update every thirty minutes. Tell them the police are involved and we're doing everything we can to find her right away." Detective McElroy turned to the other parents. "Half of you need to stay here—the lodge is home base. Keep the other students calm. No one leaves the lodge, understand? The rest of the chaperones need to serve on the search party. Mrs. Hudson, where's your phone? I'm going to call the local police."

The air in the room charged with tension as the adults went to work.

"*Ohmigosh*," whimpered Amanda. "What if—what if Shawn is out there in this storm, all alone in the cold?" She bit her lip to keep from crying.

"We've got to help with the search party," Molly said, jumping to her feet. "I want to go now."

"Sit down, Molly," Mrs. Ross said in a voice that was both gentle and firm. "None of the students will be searching outside for Shawn tonight. And the police will probably want to talk to you girls, too, since you're Shawn's best friends. I know you're worried. But we all need to stay calm." She patted Molly and Amanda's shoulders.

Natasha looked at Mrs. Ross gratefully, and, for the first time, was glad her mother had come on the trip.

An hour later, the areas around Chestnut Hill Farm were swarming with police and rescue volunteers. The police quickly converted the dining hall into search-party central; in the rec room, the students sat together in small groups, talking quietly. No one could believe that Shawn Jordan was missing.

The Chef Girls were allowed to stay with Mrs. Ross in the dining room, waiting to hear any news.

"Molls," Amanda said quietly. "I'm so worried. Waiting is awful."

"I know," Molly replied. "I just keep hoping, over and over, that—" She stopped speaking as Angie slipped into the dining room, looking ill.

Amanda stood up. "What do *you* want?" she demanded. "Shouldn't you be off celebrating somewhere?"

Angie looked pale, and her eyes were red and glassy, as if she'd been crying. "I—I need to talk to someone about Shawn," she said in a quavering voice. "I—I know what happened."

"Oh, yeah, right," Amanda said, her voice rising. "I'm sure you do, Angie."

Mrs. Ross intervened. "What's going on?" she asked.

"Tell Angie to get out," Amanda said harshly. Molly put her hand on her sister's arm, trying to calm her.

"Wait! I know where Shawn is," Angie burst out. "At least, I think I do. I think she's on Five Point."

"Why would Shawn go there?" Molly asked incredulously.

"Because I told her to!" Angie exclaimed, then burst into tears. Sobbing, she continued, "I told her Amanda had an accident on the slope. She hurried off to sit with her while I got help. And no-nobody's seen her since."

The twins stood there, shocked. "How could you?" Amanda asked, her voice trembling. "How *could* you?"

Angie started crying harder.

"Detective McElroy!" Mrs. Ross called out. "Mrs. Lopez!" She put her hand on Angie's back and quickly led her across the room. "Girls, sit there. I'll be right back," she called over her shoulder.

Molly felt sick. "Poor Shawn," she breathed. "She's been out there—in the cold—in the snow—for hours!"

"Maybe she's not outside," Natasha said nervously. "Maybe she's..." Her voice trailed off.

Everyone knew Shawn was outside.

Peichi just stared out the window at the swirling snow, her face pale.

When Amanda spoke again, her voice was hard and cold. "I'm going to get Angie for this. She'll pay."

"Yes, she will," Mrs. Ross said as she joined the group. "She'll be severely disciplined by the school. And she'll have to live for the rest of her life knowing what she did. But you don't need to get even with her, Amanda."

"But I want to! I will!" Amanda cried. "This is the most—the terrible—*what if they don't find her?*"

"Shh, shh," Mrs. Ross said comfortingly. She pulled Amanda to her. "They'll find her. She'll be okay."

"We have to get out there!" Molly said. "We have got to find her!"

Amanda started to cry softly into Mrs. Ross's shoulder.

"Come here, Molly," Mrs. Ross said. "She'll be okay." She reached out and put her other arm around Molly. "She'll be okay."

I'm so glad Mom is here, Natasha thought as she watched her mother comfort Molly and Amanda. *She knows just what to do.* Natasha reached out and touched Peichi's arm. Peichi looked at her and smiled weakly, her eyes filled with tears. There was nothing to do but wait.

chapter 11

The girls sat with Mrs. Ross in silence. After a while, it was impossible to tell how much time had passed. The search for Shawn took a different direction as Detective McElroy instructed everyone to canvass Five Point slope. Mrs. Hudson brought dozens of cups of cocoa for the students and volunteers, but Molly, Amanda, Peichi, and Natasha were too upset to drink it.

"Girls," Mrs. Ross finally said. "It will be lights out soon. There's not much you can do here while we wait. I promise that I'll wake you up if there's any news."

"Please, Mom," Natasha spoke up. "We want to stay up."

Mrs. Ross sighed. "I think it would be best for you to get a good night's—"

"They found her!"

Mr. Hudson, beaming, stood in the doorway. "They found her!" he repeated. "She's cold and upset, but okay. They'll be here in about twenty minutes."

The room erupted into cheers of joy. Everyone started hugging and talking at once.

"Oh, thank goodness," Mrs. Ross exclaimed, wiping away tears of relief. "I'll call Shawn's dad."

116

"I can't wait to see her!" Amanda said. "I was so worried!"

"Me, too," Peichi said. "I was totally freaked out! I couldn't even let myself think about what might have happened 'cause I would just get all scared and feel like I couldn't breathe, but *ohmigosh*, guys, she's okay!"

"Peichi, you barely spoke for, like, three hours!" Molly teased her friend happily.

"I know! I was so *worried*! I guess I was just saving it all up!" Peichi exclaimed. "I can't wait to see Shawn! Oh, wow, I've never been so worried in my entire life!"

The girls started laughing; they were so relieved, that suddenly everything seemed funny.

A few minutes later, Detective McElroy carried Shawn into the lodge, followed by several other volunteers. Again, the room was filled with loud cheers.

"Shawn! Shawn!" yelled Molly and Amanda as they ran over to her. Peichi and Natasha followed on their heels.

"Shawn needs a little space, girls," Detective McElroy said kindly. But before he could continue, Shawn interrupted him.

"No, they can come," she said, smiling weakly.

"You got it, Shawn," Detective McElroy replied.

Mrs. Hudson brought them to a small room on the second floor of the lodge. After she left, Molly, Amanda, Shawn, and Peichi started talking all at once.

"Are you okay? Do you feel all right?"

"We were so, so worried!"

"Angie confessed and she's in serious trouble!"

Shawn grinned weakly at her friends. "I'm freezing! And hungry! And I was really scared, too. When I heard people yelling my name on the mountain, I started crying."

Mrs. Hudson returned with a bowl of hot soup. She was followed by Mrs. Ross and a woman the twins didn't know. "This is Dr. Streick," Mrs. Hudson explained. "She needs to examine Shawn."

During Shawn's examination, the other Chef Girls waited in the hall.

Afterwards, Mrs. Ross opened the door. "Dr. Streick is done," she said. "Shawn would like you to come back in."

Shawn had changed into a bright orange sweat suit that belonged to Mrs. Hudson. Her feet and hands were bare, but the rest of her was covered with heavy blankets. Even though the room was incredibly warm, she was shivering uncontrollably.

"What's going on? Is everything okay?" Molly asked.

But Shawn only shook her head, her teeth chattering.

"She has a touch of frostbite," Dr. Streick explained, returning to the room with two basins of warm water. "It's not too bad. Now, Shawn, honey, this will be painful," Dr. Streick warned. "We've got to warm up your skin and get the blood flowing in your feet and hands." She gently slipped Shawn's foot, which was a funny grayish color, into the basin of water.

Shawn gasped. *"Oh!"* She bit her lip. "Oh, it's like the worst pins and needles I've ever had! Oh, it really hurts!"

Mrs. Ross hurried over and put her arm around Shawn as Dr. Streick dipped Shawn's other foot into the basin. "Sweetie, I just got off the phone with your father," she said, trying to distract Shawn from the pain. "He can't wait to see you. He loves you so much! He wants to drive up here right now, but it's so late that we told him to stay home. And I talked to Mr. D.—he says you can ride on the Chef Girls' bus tomorrow. Won't that be fun?"

Shawn nodded bravely, trying not to cry as Dr. Streick slowly lowered her hands into another basin of water. "J-Just as long as I d-don't have to see Angie," Shawn said. "I never want to see her again."

"Well, you won't have to see her on the trip, at least," Mrs. Ross said. "She's spending the night in the lodge, away from the other kids, and will be driven home by one of the chaperones first thing in the morning."

"Really?" the twins exclaimed together.

"She's in very serious trouble," Mrs. Ross said, nodding.

After an hour, Shawn's toes and fingers had returned to their normal color, though they still felt tender. She yawned loudly. "Sorry. I'm so tired."

"Well, you've been through so much!" Mrs. Ross said kindly. "We're all exhausted. Mr. Hudson brought his

119

truck up to the front of the lodge, so you wouldn't have to walk back in the cold."

"Everyone is taking such good care of me," Shawn said with a smile.

"We're just so happy you're okay!" Mrs. Ross said as she helped Shawn to her feet. "Come on, girls, it's time for bed. No staying up late tonight, okay?"

"No problem," yawned Peichi, and everyone chuckled.

By the next morning, over six inches of snow had fallen. Mr. Hudson and other staff members had been up for most of the night, plowing local roads. On their way to breakfast, the Chef Girls saw three buses pulled up in front of the lodge. "Well, I guess the trip is really over," Amanda said. "I'm kind of ready to go back home."

"Me, too," Molly said. "Last night was so horrible! I'm ready for things to get back to normal."

"I'm kind of worried they won't," Shawn said nervously. "At least, not for a while. I'm afraid everyone's gonna treat me differently. Like they did after—after my mom died."

The twins nodded. "They might," Molly said seriously. "It was such a scary thing—I mean, it was horrible for you, Shawn—but everyone was really freaked out."

"And I just don't know what's going to happen with the whole Angie thing," Shawn sighed.

"Let's not think about it," Natasha spoke up. "It's our last meal at the lodge! And we're all riding home together—the way it should be! I think we'll have a blast!"

But in the dining room, the other students were quiet and subdued. People stared at Shawn so much that she could hardly eat her breakfast.

"I wish everyone would stop looking at me!" Shawn whispered to her friends. "It's totally weird."

"I have an idea," Molly spoke up. A mischievous smile crept over her face as she climbed onto her chair.

"Molly! What are you doing!"

"Okay, listen up, everybody," Molly called out. The dining room grew silent. "This is Shawn. She's back safe and sound. If you want to come talk to her, that's cool. But don't just stare at her. That's totally creepy. Thank you!"

As Molly sat down, the girls burst into giggles. "I can't believe you did that!" Natasha exclaimed.

Molly shrugged. "Somebody had to," she said.

"Thanks, Molly," Shawn said gratefully.

An hour later, the girls waved good-bye to Mr. and Mrs. Hudson as they boarded Bus #1.

"Was everyone this quiet on the ride up?" Shawn asked as the bus lumbered down the road.

"Nope," Molly replied. "I think everybody is tired. All the skiing, the staying up late—"

"Look! Up in the air! It's a bird! It's a plane! It's Super-Moose!" Omar's voice boomed through the bus.

"Oh, no," Peichi moaned, shrinking down in her seat as Omar waved her battered stuffed animal in the air. It was wearing a red T-shirt like a cape!

Omar tossed Moosie to the front of the bus. The kid who caught Moosie threw him back, and soon the entire bus was making Moosie fly through the air like a super-hero. Even Peichi had to laugh as Omar made crazy sound effects whenever Moosie soared through the air.

"Stop! I demand you cease and desist from this animal cruelty!" Omar suddenly yelled out. "Don't worry, Sir Moose, I'll rescue you!" Omar jumped out of his seat and leaped into the air to grab Moosie as he flew past. Then Omar charged down the aisle to Peichi's seat.

"Lady Peichi, I return to you Sir Moose, safe from harm and full of exciting tales of bravery and danger," Omar announced in a goofy voice as he kneeled in the aisle. "No thanks necessary, really, it was my pleasure, anytime you need anything, I'm your man." As Peichi reached out to take her moose, Omar suddenly grabbed her hand. "Mwa!" he smacked a kiss on her hand, then charged back down the aisle to his seat.

The bus full of kids cracked up.

"Ewww!" Peichi wiped off her hand, pretending to be completely disgusted. But her friends could tell from her goofy grin that she didn't really mind.

Shawn sat back and grinned at her friends. "Manda, you were right," she said. "This *is* the good bus."

Several hours later, the buses pulled up in front of Windsor Middle School. Dozens of parents were standing in front of the school, chatting and drinking coffee.

"It feels like we were away for a really long time," Peichi said. "But it was only four days! Isn't that weird?"

Shawn nodded. "I can't wait to see my dad," she said. "Oh! There he is!" As soon as the door opened, Shawn jumped out of her seat and pushed her way down the aisle. "Dad!" she yelled as her father looked at the kids streaming out of each bus, searching for her. "Dad!"

When Mr. Jordan saw Shawn, his face lit up. She ran into his arms. "Shawn, Shawn," he said. "Baby, I was so worried. I'm so glad you're okay."

"I love you, Dad," Shawn said as her father squeezed her tight.

"I love you so much, baby," Mr. Jordan replied. "You're my little girl."

We're all we've got, Shawn thought as she hugged her dad again and again. *If anything ever happened to me, Dad would be all alone. And if anything ever happened to him...*Shawn put the terrible thought out of her mind and buried her head in her dad's chest. "I love you, Dad," she said again.

123

"Let's get your bag and go home," Mr. Jordan said.

Just then, Principal Wagner approached them. "Shawn, we're so glad you're all right," she said warmly. "Mr. Jordan, I'm sure you're eager to take Shawn home. But would you mind stepping into my office for a moment? I'd like a word with you both."

As Shawn and her father followed Principal Wagner into the school, a feeling of dread came over Shawn as she remembered all the horrible things Angie had done to her over the past months. *I don't want to come back here ever again,* she thought. *I can't handle being in the same building with Angie every single day.*

Once again, Shawn found herself sitting in Principal Wagner's office.

"First, I want you to know that Angie has been suspended for the next two weeks," Principal Wagner said. "We'll consider expulsion if she ever bullies Shawn again, but I'm hopeful that the girls' problems can be resolved without such drastic measures."

"Problems?" Mr. Jordan asked, raising his eyebrows. "Shawn and Angie haven't been having problems. They had a falling-out last spring, but that's it."

"Actually, Dad," Shawn said, "Angie really, really hates me. She's been pretty awful. I didn't say anything because I kind of thought she'd get sick of picking on me sooner or later. But she's just gotten meaner."

Mr. Jordan and Principal Wagner listened quietly as

Shawn told them about everything—the horrible things Angie had said, the hang-up phone calls, the graffiti on her locker.

"Shawn! Why didn't you tell me about this?" Mr. Jordan asked, shocked.

"I didn't want to make things worse," Shawn explained. "I thought Angie would just get sick of picking on me."

"There's an excellent technique for dealing with bullying called mediation," Principal Wagner said. "A counselor would come to the school for a private session with Shawn and Angie to help them resolve their differences."

"I don't have any differences with Angie," Shawn spoke up. "It's just that I never want to see her again."

"I understand, Shawn," Principal Wagner said, nodding her head. "But you two do attend the same school, and are both members of the cheerleading squad. You will see her again, unless one of you switches schools. Mediation is a confidential opportunity for you and Angie to try to work through your problems. You don't have to do anything you don't want to do, Shawn, but Angie and her mother are very open to this."

Shawn thought for a minute. "Would my dad be there?"

"Not in the room, unfortunately," Principal Wagner replied. "But he can wait right outside. You can think about it for a few days, if you'd like."

"No, that's okay," Shawn said. "I'll do it. I'll do anything to make Angie stop." Suddenly, Shawn felt very, very tired.

I just want to go home and curl up in bed, she thought.

"Shawn, that's great," Principal Wagner replied. "Are you two free on Wednesday afternoon? I'd like to set this up as soon as possible."

"I am," Mr. Jordan replied, looking at Shawn. She nodded.

"Mr. Jordan, here's my card," Principal Wagner said. "Please call me if you have any questions. Shawn, you look exhausted. Rest up and take care—if you need to stay home from school tomorrow, that's fine."

"Shawn's going to the doctor tomorrow morning," Mr. Jordan replied. "I'll probably keep her home for the rest of the day."

Principal Wagner walked Shawn and Mr. Jordan to the front of the school. "Shawn, we're all so glad that you're okay. I know you've been through a lot lately, and I want you to know that it's going to stop now. My door is always open for you. If Angie or anyone else gives you trouble, *please* let me know right away."

"Thank you," Shawn said quietly, blinking back tears.

"You're safe at Windsor Middle School. We want you to learn here, and have fun here. We won't let anyone get in the way of that."

"I appreciate that, Mrs. Wagner," Mr. Jordan replied. "We both do."

"See you on Wednesday, Shawn," Principal Wagner said with a smile.

$\mathcal{S}$hawn was glad that she got to stay home from school on Tuesday. After her doctor's appointment, she worked on her blue painting, and then took a long nap. When she woke, she was surprised to find her dad in his office, working on his new book.

"Hey, Dad," Shawn said with a yawn. "Don't you have to teach classes today?"

"I cancelled my classes," Mr. Jordan explained with a smile. "I wanted to be here in case you need anything."

"Oh. Thanks," Shawn said. "Actually, I do need something—lunch. I'm really hungry!"

Mr. Jordan laughed. "Me, too! Mrs. Moore stopped by while you were asleep. The twins made a big pot of matzoh ball soup for you!"

"Wow—that was so nice of them," Shawn exclaimed. "I love their matzoh ball soup!"

"Mrs. Moore was so relieved to hear that you were okay," Mr. Jordan said as he heated the soup. "She's taking the twins shopping for dresses for Natasha's bat mitzvah this afternoon and was wondering if we wanted to come along—if you're up to it."

"Really? Even though I didn't go to school today?" Shawn asked. "Awesome!"

"Well, there is one condition—you have to finish this big bowl of soup first," Mr. Jordan teased. "So eat up!"

A few hours later, Shawn and her dad met Molly, Amanda, and Mrs. Moore in the Juniors' department of Macy's. Mrs. Moore gave Shawn a big hug.

"What did I miss at school?" Shawn asked the twins.

"Well, everyone was talking about you," Amanda said. "But not in a bad way. They were saying what an evil witch Angie is, and how she's totally jealous of you because you are way cooler than she could, like, ever hope to be."

"Really?"

"Yup. And everyone was worried when you stayed home, but Molls and I told them you were okay. You're, like, a celebrity now!"

"And everyone's talking about how Angie got suspended for two weeks!" Molly added. "I don't think she should even bother coming back to school."

"What kind of dresses are you guys looking for?" Shawn asked, changing the subject quickly. The last thing she wanted to talk about was Angie.

"I asked Natasha and she said that we should wear a nice outfit to the temple, but a fancy dress to the party that night! Let's get in there and start shopping!" Amanda exclaimed.

The twins and Shawn combed the racks with Mrs. Moore, while Mr. Jordan stood back and watched. Soon, they had several beautiful dresses to try on.

"Come on, let's hit the dressing room!" Amanda said.

Giggling, the twins and Shawn helped one another try on the dresses. Molly liked the first one she tried on—a navy satin dress with short sleeves and a straight skirt. Amanda and Shawn had a little more difficulty picking out their dresses.

"You guys look great in all of them," Molly pointed out. "Shawn, that red one looks really nice on you. And Amanda, you love the lacy one. Why don't you try them on again and we'll ask Mom and Mr. Jordan?"

"Good idea, Molly," said Shawn.

"Yeah—who knew Molls would ever give fashion advice?" Amanda joked.

Shawn slipped into a ruby-colored velvet dress that had spaghetti straps and a flared skirt. Amanda picked a cream-colored lace slip dress that had tiny, off-the-shoulder sleeves. "This isn't what I thought I'd get," she said. "But I love it!"

The girls hurried out of the dressing room to show their parents.

"You look *stunning*," said Mrs. Moore. "Oh, you're all growing up!"

129

"I think you three picked the most beautiful dresses in the place," Mr. Jordan added with a grin.

That night, Shawn couldn't sleep. *I don't want to go back to school tomorrow,* she realized. *I wish I hadn't said I'd do the mediation thing. What if Angie's really terrible to me? I don't want to be anywhere near her.*

She slipped out of bed and walked to her closet to look at her new dress, but it didn't make her feel better. *I missed Mom so much today,* Shawn thought. *I miss her more and more. It's not getting easier.*

Shawn turned off the light and crawled back into bed. *I don't want to start crying again,* she thought angrily. *I've been crying too much lately! Enough, already!*

But she couldn't stop the tears.

After school the next day, Shawn met her father at the main office. To her relief, Angie wasn't there yet.

"Hi, baby," he said warmly when she walked in. "How was school today?"

"Good. Better than I thought it would be," Shawn replied. "People treated me pretty normally."

Miss Hinkle smiled at Shawn over her funny, old-fashioned half-glasses. "Ms. Martinez just called—they're running late and will be here in about ten minutes."

Angie's always late, Shawn thought. *Guess her mom is, too.* Shawn tried to ignore the queasy feeling in her stomach.

Mr. Jordan leaned over and whispered, "You don't have to do this if you don't want to, Shawn," as if he knew what she was feeling.

"Thanks, Dad," Shawn told him. "But I just want to get it over with."

A few minutes later, the door opened and Angie and Ms. Martinez entered. With an ugly scowl on her face, Angie sat at the opposite end of the bench from Shawn.

Ms. Martinez was a very thin woman with blonde hair pulled into a tight ponytail. She marched up to the desk to tell Miss Hinkle they had arrived, then turned to Shawn and Mr. Jordan. "I'm very sorry for how Angie has behaved," she said coldly. "She's been severely punished." Then Ms. Martinez sat next to Angie. They both ignored each other.

Poor Angie, Shawn thought. *Ms. Martinez seems so mean. And she's all that Angie has.*

"Shawn? Angie? Right this way, please."

A middle-aged woman with long, curly red hair stood in the doorway. Her gray eyes were kind as she smiled at Shawn and Angie.

Here we go, Shawn thought, feeling her heart beat

faster. She and Angie followed the woman to a small conference room next to Principal Wagner's office. Shawn could see Principal Wagner at her desk, and felt better knowing that she was close by.

"My name is Jill Newman," said the woman as everyone sat down. "I'm a counselor trained in mediation. My job is to help people work through their problems to find a solution that makes everyone happy. And that's what I'd like to do with you today.

"Before we begin, I'd like to go over some ground rules," Jill continued. "First, this is a safe space—no name-calling, no threats, no yelling. Second, if anyone needs a break, we can take a time-out. Third, everything that happens in this room is confidential. You cannot talk about it with anyone else. Understand?"

Shawn and Angie nodded.

"Good. Now, Principal Wagner told me that you two used to be good friends. Angie, how did you and Shawn become friends?"

Angie looked surprised. "Um, we're both cheerleaders," she said. "Shawn was cool. We got along really well. Uh, we had a lot of fun together."

Jill nodded. "Good. Shawn, do you agree with that?"

"Yeah. And, uh, Angie and I had a lot in common. When my dad started dating last year, she'd been through it with her mom. She understood exactly how I felt. And I had fun hanging out with her." Shawn looked down as she remembered how close she and Angie had been.

"But something happened to change all of that. Can you tell me about it?"

After a pause, Shawn spoke. "I started thinking that maybe Angie and I didn't have so much in common. One time, she stole gum from a store. That made me nervous. And she was always mean to my other friends. Then..."

"Go on," Jill encouraged.

"I saw Angie do something really harsh to another girl on the cheerleading squad," Shawn finished. "And I just didn't want to be friends with somebody who could do that. I didn't want to fight with her. I just didn't trust her anymore."

"Actually, the problem is more that Shawn became this big snob," Angie interrupted. "She started acting like she was too *good* for me. I was all, *whatever*."

"Okay, let's remember, no name-calling," Jill said gently. "It's always sad when a friendship ends, isn't it? Unfortunately, it's a part of life that people change and start needing different things from their friends. Normally, though, the end of a friendship doesn't lead to such trouble. I'd like to talk about that now. What happened?"

"Angie just started hating me," Shawn said quietly. "I never tried to hurt her."

"Angie? Can you tell us why you started doing all these things to Shawn?" Jill asked quietly.

Angie shrugged. "I don't know."

"Angie," Jill said again. "You haven't treated Shawn very well. You need to explain why you've behaved this way."

Angie didn't say anything.

I should have known this would be a waste of time, Shawn thought angrily. *Angie will never own up to what she's done.*

"Angie, Shawn could have died this weekend," Jill continued. "I want to know why you would put someone who was your friend in such a dangerous situation. I want you to explain to us why you've treated Shawn so cruelly."

Still, Angie remained silent. Then Shawn heard her sniff. *Ohmigosh,* Shawn thought. *I've never seen Angie cry before.*

Jill pushed a box of tissues over to Angie. "Angie, remember that you're in a safe space here," she said. "What are you thinking about?"

"Shawn was my best friend," Angie said quietly as she wiped the tears from her face. "And then she just—she didn't want anything to do with me anymore. I missed her a lot. And then I got really mad. She just dropped me. What kind of friend would do that?

"It felt like when my dad left. One day, everything seemed fine. Then he was packing his suitcase and I kept asking him to take me with him. But he didn't. He just left. And I never saw him again." Angie put her head on the table and her shoulders started to shake with silent sobs.

"Angie, I didn't mean to just ditch you," Shawn said. "I didn't think I could be a very good friend. It seemed like we were too different." As Angie continued to cry, Shawn felt a lump in her throat. "Angie, I miss my mom, too," she said. "I miss her every day. I miss her so much that it hurts." She blinked hard, trying to keep from crying.

"You're both very brave girls," Jill spoke up. "Losing a parent is one of the most painful experiences you will ever endure. And the loss can stay with you forever. I think that one of the reasons you became such good friends so quickly was because you had both experienced losing a parent."

Shawn glanced up to see Angie looking at her—but this time, Angie wasn't staring at her with a look of hatred. There was understanding in her dark brown eyes. *She knows,* Shawn thought to herself. *She knows what it's like to miss someone so much.*

"And losing a best friend can hurt terribly," Jill continued. "But bullying Shawn won't make you feel better, Angie. You don't look like you feel better."

"I don't," Angie said. "I felt *awful* this weekend when I found out Shawn was missing."

"I'd like to write up a contract for you both to sign," Jill said. "The contract will have certain rules for behavior to keep this from happening again. Is that okay?"

After Shawn and Angie nodded, Jill left the room. Shawn cleared her throat. "Detective McElroy told me that if you hadn't come forward, it would have taken them a lot longer to find me. I wanted to thank you for doing that."

"I'm really sorry, Shawn," Angie said. "I never meant for it to go so far."

"I'm sorry, too," Shawn replied. And she was sorry— sorry that Angie had been so hurt when Shawn had ended their friendship. As Shawn and Angie waited quietly for Jill to return with the contract, Shawn knew that she and Angie would never be friends again; too much had happened between them.

But she also knew that they would no longer be enemies.

When Shawn and her dad got home that afternoon, she told him she had something to show him. "I've been working on this painting for a little while," Shawn said shyly. "It's not finished yet..."

Her father silently looked at the portrait Shawn had painted of her mom. "Baby, it's beautiful," he finally said. "What made you use all different shades of blue?"

Shawn shrugged. "Blue is a sad color," she said simply. "But it can also feel quiet and peaceful. I've been missing Mom a lot. And the blue matches my feelings."

"Shawn," Mr. Jordan began, "we haven't talked about Mom in a while. But you can talk to me whenever you want—you know that, right?"

Shawn nodded and smiled sadly at her dad.

"Maybe you'd like to talk to someone else, too," Mr. Jordan said. "A counselor like Jill?"

Shawn thought for a moment, then nodded again. "Going to counseling right after Mom died helped a lot. But now that I'm older...I guess I miss her in different ways."

"I do, too," Mr. Jordan said heavily. "All the time." He was silent for a moment, then said, "I'll make an appointment for you to see someone next week."

Shawn reached up and hugged her dad.

"What a hard time you've been having, baby girl," Mr. Jordan said as he kissed the top of Shawn's head. "My brave little girl..."

"Everyone keeps saying that, but I don't feel very brave, Dad. I've just been crying all the time."

"That's okay, baby," Mr. Jordan replied. "Sometimes, crying is the best way to get your feelings out. It's going to get better. I promise it will."

Shawn looked into her father's warm brown eyes and knew, in her heart, that he was right.

chapter 13

Today is my bat mitzvah! Natasha thought as soon as she woke up on Saturday morning. She sat up in bed, feeling more excited than anxious as she thought of the day ahead of her—the solemn ceremony at the temple in the morning, the fabulous party her parents had planned for that night. *This is going to be the most amazing day of my life!*

Natasha quickly showered and went down to the kitchen, where her parents were eating breakfast. At first, Natasha felt too nervous to eat, but realized how hungry she was after her first bite of cornflakes. After breakfast, Natasha returned to her room to put on her new outfit, a soft blue wool dress with long sleeves and embroidery at the hem. She looked at the shimmery lavender dress she would wear for the party that night and felt a shiver of excitement. *I'm so glad Connor is coming tonight! I hope he asks me to dance!*

There was a soft knock at the door, and Mrs. Ross entered. "Oh, Natasha," she said proudly. "You look lovely."

"Thanks, Mom," Natasha replied shyly.

"Before my bat mitzvah, my mother gave me this necklace," Mrs. Ross said, placing her hand on the silver

Star of David that she always wore. It had a tiny diamond on each point. "You are my jewel, Natasha, my precious daughter. Today, you will become a woman in the eyes of our faith. This necklace belongs to you now."

"Oh, Mom. It's so beautiful," Natasha breathed. "Thank you so much."

Mrs. Ross fastened the necklace around Natasha's neck and gave her a hug. "Are you ready, sweetheart?" she asked. "It's time to go."

A few minutes later, Natasha and her parents arrived at Temple Beth-El, a large brick building with tall, narrow windows and a domed roof. Rabbi Perlman met them in the foyer. "Welcome, welcome!" he exclaimed. "Natasha's big day is finally here. Come with me—I'll get you settled while we wait for the rest of the congregants to arrive."

In a small anteroom outside the sanctuary (the main room of the synagogue), Mr. Ross squeezed Natasha's hand gently. "Princess, you're going to be great!"

"Thanks, Dad," Natasha said, starting to feel more nervous. *Relax*, she told herself as she took a deep breath. *You've been planning for this for years! It'll be okay.*

"Natasha, honey, you know exactly what to do," Mrs. Ross whispered in her ear. "I was anxious before my bat mitzvah, too. But it will be over before you know it!"

Natasha smiled at her mother, then pictured her

friends sitting together on one of the dark wooden benches in the sanctuary.

Suddenly, it was time for the service to begin. Natasha sat with her parents at the *bimah*, the front stage area of the sanctuary. Behind her, Rabbi Perlman led the congregation in prayer. Then he removed the Torah scrolls from the ark, the special cupboard in which they were kept.

Then Rabbi Perlman gestured for Natasha to join him at the wooden pedestal on which he had carefully placed the Torah scrolls.

This is it, Natasha thought as she took a deep breath. She began singing from the Torah in Hebrew. All of her practicing paid off—the words came naturally to her, and as Natasha grew more confident, her voice rang out clearly and sweetly through the temple.

There was silence in the sanctuary when Natasha finished. She looked at everyone seated in the sanctuary and spotted the Chef Girls smiling at her. She smiled back as she began to speak.

"My portion of the Torah relates to service. Serving others is very important in the Jewish religion, and I learned how important it is almost by accident. I love to cook, and my friends and I have a cooking business. But from the very beginning of our business, helping others has been one of the most important things we do. We've helped out with a charity fund-raiser for people suffering from hunger. We've given food to a family who just had a baby, and to a family that suffered through a fire in their apartment." Natasha paused and looked around the sanctuary. "Food is such a basic thing for most of us. It's easy to forget that people in our community, our neighbors, sometimes need help. In happy times and in sad times, it's important to be there for everyone in the community."

Before she knew it, the hard part was over—and she had enjoyed it!

The rest of the ceremony passed by quickly. Natasha beamed as her parents spoke to the congregation about how proud they were of her. Then Mr. and Mrs. Ross recited a blessing, and suddenly Natasha realized, *It's over— my bat mitzvah is over! I didn't mess up!* She had never felt so happy—or relieved—in her entire life.

"*Wow,*" Amanda said in awe as she and Molly entered the ballroom of the Palace Hotel later that evening. "This is the fanciest place we've ever been!"

"Seriously," Molly agreed. "I hope I don't spill anything."

The elegant room was decorated in ivory and gold. Sparkling chandeliers hung from the ceiling, and pale purple roses graced each table. Men in tuxedos and women in formal dresses milled about, chatting and laughing. A long buffet table was crowded with dozens of dishes, and at the far end of the room, a live band was setting up next to a gleaming parquet dance floor.

"Molly! Amanda!" Peichi called as she and Shawn hurried over to the twins. "Can you believe this place? Everything is so fancy and gorgeous! It's amazing! This is gonna be the best party ever! I can't wait to hit the dance floor! And the buffet! That food looks *delicious*! *Ohmigosh*, did you see Omar? He looks so funny in his suit! Actually, all the guys do! It's so weird to see them wearing something besides jeans!"

"Hey, Chef Girls!" Natasha said happily as she came up to her friends. "I'm so glad you're here."

"Natasha, congratulations!" Amanda said, giving her friend a hug. "You did great today."

"You look great, too," Shawn added. "Your dress is gorgeous!"

"Thanks! You all look amazing, too," Natasha replied, beaming. "Come on, let's find the photographer! I want a picture with my best friends!"

After dinner, the Chef Girls danced for an hour as the band played lots of fun music. The dance floor was crowded with people of all ages, everyone dancing together.

"Phew! I need to take a break," Amanda said, panting. "And I *really* need a piece of that cake. It looks *sooo* yummy."

"Let's all go," Peichi said.

But when they reached the dessert table, the band started playing a slow song. Connor and Omar walked up to the girls.

"Hey, Natasha," Connor said shyly. "Um, would you like to dance?"

Natasha's face lit up. "Sure!" she replied. She grinned at her friends as she followed Connor back onto the dance floor.

"Hey, Cheng," Omar called. "I don't have anything better to do—wanna dance?"

"With you?" Peichi asked, looking like she was about to crack a joke. Then, suddenly, she seemed to change her mind. "Um, okay." Her friends could tell she was trying

not to giggle as she and Omar started slow dancing.

"Wow, that was fast," Amanda said lightly. "Justin will probably be over any minute to ask you to dance, Molls."

Molly shrugged. "I don't feel like dancing right now. I'd rather hang out with you guys."

"I know what you mean," Amanda said seriously. "This cake looks too good to pass up just to dance with some boy."

"*Mmm*, this cake *is* really good!" Shawn exclaimed after her first bite. "It's so rich."

Molly looked thoughtful as she chewed a bite of

cake. "The frosting is amazing. What's that flavor? I can tell they blended strawberries into the frosting, but there's something else, too."

"I think it's got a lot of vanilla in it," Amanda said. "You guys! We should try to make this frosting! It would taste awesome on cupcakes. We could make them for Dish. And speaking of Dish, we need to book a *lot* of jobs so I can pay back Mom and Dad for the ski trip."

"Great idea, Amanda," Shawn said. "I bet our clients would love cupcakes with this frosting."

"Maybe we can sneak a piece of cake home, to make sure we have the flavors right," Amanda said thoughtfully.

Molly raised her eyebrows, and Shawn started laughing.

"What?" Amanda asked. "I'm doing this for our *business*, guys!"

"And for your sweet tooth, Manda," Molly teased her sister.

Shawn grinned. Laughing with her best friends, eating the delicious cake, having a ball at the best party she'd ever been to—Shawn felt happier than she had in a long time. *It may take a while for my life to feel normal again,* she thought. *But I know that my friends will always be there, no matter what happens.*

dish
The Amazing cookbook

By
The ★C★H★E★F★ Girls

AMANDA!
Molly!
Peichi ☺
shawn!
Natasha!

Cinnamon Milk

serves 1

1 ½ cups milk
1 tablespoon sugar
½ teaspoon cinnamon
⅛ teaspoon nutmeg
⅛ teaspoon vanilla
1 cinnamon stick

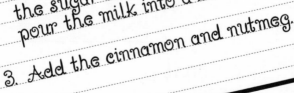

1. In a small saucepan, warm the milk over low heat.

2. Add the sugar and stir the milk constantly until the sugar dissolves. Then pour the milk into a bowl.

3. Add the cinnamon and nutmeg.

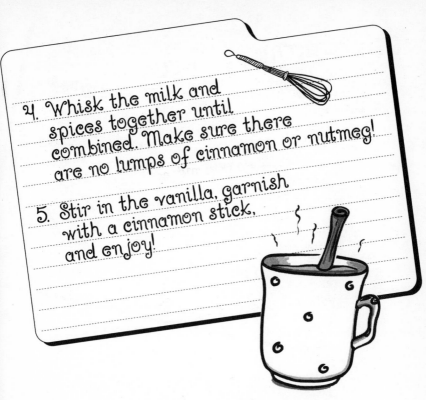

4. Whisk the milk and spices together until combined. Make sure there are no lumps of cinnamon or nutmeg!

5. Stir in the vanilla, garnish with a cinnamon stick, and enjoy!

My dad always makes this milk on cold winter nights. It's a yummy change from hot chocolate and is extra-good as a bedtime treat!

-Natasha

TACOS

1 SMALL ONION
1 POUND GROUND BEEF
2 TABLESPOONS CHILI POWDER
1 HEAD OF LETTUCE
2 LARGE TOMATOES
1 POUND CHEDDAR
    OR JACK CHEESE
    8 READY-MADE
    TACO SHELLS

OPTIONAL TOPPINGS:
SLICED OLIVES
SOUR CREAM
SALSA
GUACAMOLE

1. CHOP THE ONION AND SAUTÉ IT IN A SMALL AMOUNT OF OIL IN A LARGE FRYING PAN. ADD THE GROUND BEEF AND CHILI POWDER. COOK OVER MEDIUM HEAT UNTIL THE GROUND BEEF IS DONE. YOU CAN ADD MORE CHILI POWDER IF YOU WANT TO GIVE YOUR TACOS EXTRA KICK! SET ASIDE.

2. PREPARE THE TOPPINGS: WASH AND SHRED THE LETTUCE, WASH AND CHOP THE TOMATOES, AND SHRED THE CHEESE.

MOM MAKES AWESOME TACOS. THEY ARE FUN
TO SERVE AT A PARTY, BECAUSE EVERYBODY
CAN ADD THEIR OWN TOPPINGS!

—AMANDA

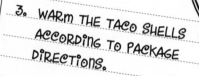

3. WARM THE TACO SHELLS
   ACCORDING TO PACKAGE
   DIRECTIONS.

4. NOW HAVE FUN BUILDING YOUR TACOS! LAYER
   THE BEEF, LETTUCE, TOMATOES, AND CHEESE
   IN THE TACO SHELLS. TOP WITH OLIVES,
   SOUR CREAM, SALSA, AND/OR
   GUACAMOLE IF YOU WANT.
   EVERYONE WILL WANT SECONDS!

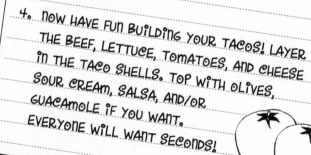

Snowshoe Chicken

serves 4

½ cup maple syrup

¼ cup water

3 tablespoons Dijon mustard

3 tablespoons balsamic vinegar

1 teaspoon black pepper

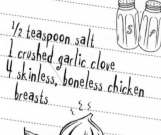

½ teaspoon salt

1 crushed garlic clove

4 skinless, boneless chicken breasts

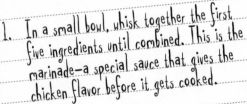

1. In a small bowl, whisk together the first five ingredients until combined. This is the marinade—a special sauce that gives the chicken flavor before it gets cooked.

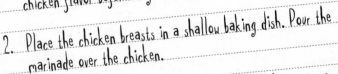

2. Place the chicken breasts in a shallow baking dish. Pour the marinade over the chicken.

3. Refrigerate the chicken and marinade for 2-4 hours, turning every 30 minutes so that both sides get coated with marinade.

This was the first meal we had at Chestnut Hill Farm. Mrs. Hudson gave us the recipe. I don't know why they call it Snowshoe Chicken, but the maple-mustard sauce is really yummy!

—Peichi

4. When you're ready to cook the chicken, place the chicken breasts in a large frying pan over medium heat.

It's very important to THROW AWAY ANY EXTRA MARINADE!!!

5. Cook the chicken for 6–8 minutes on each side or until done. Yum!

cooking tips from the chef Girls!

The Chef Girls are looking out for you!
Here are some things you should
know if you want to cook.
(Remember to ask your parents
if you can use knives and the stove!)

1   Tie back long hair so that it won't
    get into the food or in the way as
    you work.

2   Don't wear loose-fitting clothing
    that could drag in the food or
    on the stove burners.

3   Never cook in bare feet or open-toed
    shoes. Something sharp or hot could
    drop on your feet.

4   Always wash your hands before you
    handle food.

5   Read through the recipe before you start. Gather your ingredients together and measure them before you begin.

6   Turn pot handles in so that they won't get knocked off the stove.

7   Use wooden spoons to stir hot liquids. Metal spoons can become very hot.

8   When cutting or peeling food, cut away from your hands.

9   Cut food on a cutting board, not the countertop.

 10   Hand someone a knife with the knifepoint pointing to the floor.

11   Clean up as you go. It's safer and neater.

12   Always use a dry pot holder to remove something hot from the oven. You could get burned with a wet one, since wet ones retain heat.

13   Make sure that any spills on the floor are cleaned up right away, so that you don't slip and fall.

14 Don't put knives in clean-up water. You could reach into the water and cut yourself.

15 Use a wire rack to cool hot baking dishes to avoid scorch marks on the countertop.

An Important Message from the Chef Girls!

Some foods can carry bacteria, such as salmonella, that can make you sick.
To avoid salmonella, always cook poultry, ground beef, and eggs thoroughly before eating.
Don't eat or drink foods containing raw eggs.
And wash hands, kitchen work surfaces, and utensils with soap and water immediately after they have been in contact with raw meat or poultry.

Instant messaging and e-mail dictionary!
diSh

mooretimes2: Molly and Amanda

qtpie490: Shawn

happyface: Peichi

BrooklynNatasha: Natasha

JustMac: Justin

Wuzzup: What's up?

Mwa smooching sound

G2G: Got To Go

deets: details

b-b: Bye-Bye

brb: be right back

<3 hearts

L8R: Later, as in "See ya later!"

LOL: Laughing Out Loud

GMTA: Great Minds Think Alike

j/k: Just kidding

B/C: because

W8: Wait

W8 4 me @: Wait for me at

thanx: thanks

BK: Big kiss

MAY: Mad about you

RUF2T?: Are you free to talk?

TTUL: Type to you later

E-ya: will e-mail you

LMK: Let me know

GR8: Great

WFM: Works for me

2: to, too, two

C: see

u: you

2morrow: tomorrow

VH: virtual hug

BFFL: Best Friends For Life

:-@ shock

:-P sticking out tongue

%-) confused

:-o surprised

;-) winking or teasing